A GIRL CALLED JOY

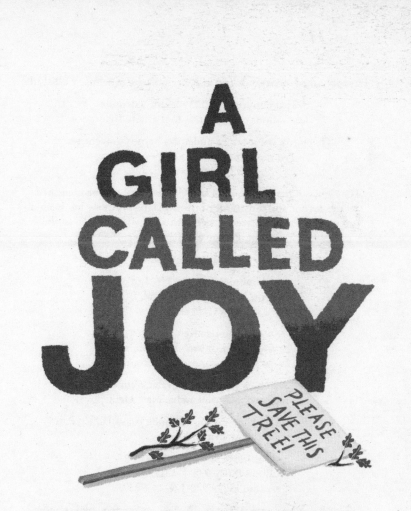

A GIRL CALLED JOY

JENNY VALENTINE

Illustrations by Claire Lefevre

SIMON & SCHUSTER

First published in Great Britain in 2021 by Simon & Schuster UK Ltd

1 3 5 7 9 10 8 6 4 2

Simon & Schuster UK Ltd
1st Floor, 222 Gray's Inn Road, London
WC1X 8HB

www.simonandschuster.co.uk
www.simonandschuster.com.au
www.simonandschuster.co.in

Simon & Schuster Australia, Sydney
Simon & Schuster India, New Delhi

A CIP catalogue record for this book is available from
the British Library.

PB ISBN 978-1-4711-9649-2
eBook ISBN 978-1-4711-9648-5
eAudio ISBN 978-1-4711-9989-9

Typeset in the UK by Sorrel Packham
Printed and bound by CPI Group (UK) Ltd, Croydon, CR0 4YY

*For optimists
everywhere*

1

There is absolutely no storybook magic in our family. We don't have a grandad who can fly, or an uncle who is busy somewhere building a time machine, or parents who are world-famous wizards-in-hiding. Our grandad walks with a stick, we have zero uncles, and our mum and dad have out-of-the-blue started saying things like, 'Put that back where it came from,' and, 'Where's your school uniform?' and,

'Please hoover your room immediately.'

According to my big sister, Claude, this makes us extremely ordinary. But we have never been ordinary. And I don't think we should be ready to start now.

I'm not pretending there haven't been some big changes. Things are feeling very pedestrian around here, that's for sure. Extremely squidged in. And it goes without saying that nobody has a wand to get us out of trouble, or their own super-helpful pack of wolves, or a lump of rock that can speak in whole sentences. There are no parallel universes under our sinks, or other worlds in our wardrobes, or perfect tiny humans between our walls. There are cleaning products, and clothes, and possibly mice. I don't have shoes that rush about all over the place with a mind of their own. I have one pair of trainers that are at least one size too small, and I am not ready to throw them away yet because they have been with me everywhere, on so many adventures. The washing machine won't get the grass stains out of Claude's precious new jeans, and right now, Dad can't get rid of the coffee he spilled on Grandad's carpet. So I am pretty sure that none of us can make stuff disappear.

But the thing is, there is more than one kind of magic. It shouldn't have to mean the same as *impossible*, and only be allowed to happen in stories. That just doesn't seem right to me. Claude says our definitions of magic are different, and that I am always marvelling at something or other for no good reason because I am way too easily impressed. I am twenty-four seven on the lookout for some everyday, actually real-life magic because that's the kind I believe in, and, to be honest, I think we could do with some.

When I say so, Claude does one of her semi-professional eye-rolls and says, 'Oh, yeah? Well. Good luck with that.'

When you don't have storybook magic, your problems are less fancy and not as much fun to fix. For example, Dad has stuck a big heavy book about trees over the coffee stain, in a hurry, and now it is lurking there in the middle of the room where it doesn't belong, like a suitcase in a canal. Any minute, somebody, most likely Grandad, is going to bump into it and find out the truth. Claude says it's not going to be pretty when he does, and it is only a matter of time. Even with my talent for positive thinking, I am starting to think she might have got that one right.

I am ten, and Claude is thirteen.

She smells like cherries and wears black make-up all over her eyes. She has the straightest, whitest teeth and the shiniest toothpaste smile I have ever seen. When she is happy, she looks like an advert for the dentist, but at the moment that isn't very often. Dad says Claude's toothpaste smile has become a bit like a meteor shower, because it might only happen once or twice a year, and if you blink you'll miss it.

We saw a meteor shower in California, when I was six and Claude was nine. The sky rained stars for hours and hours, and I fell asleep before it was finished. You would have to do a long old blink to miss that.

Claude is short for Claudia Eloise, and

rhymes with bored, which these days is just about right. Ever since we got back to the UK and moved into Grandad's house, she is always complaining that nothing is worth doing and there is less than nothing to do. Mum and Dad have started calling her *the brick wall*, but not so she can hear them. They whisper it behind their hands, but I'm not sure they need to bother. As far as I can tell, she has pretty much completely stopped listening to anything they have to say.

Mum and Dad's names are Rina and Dan, short for Marina Jane Blake and Daniel Samson Applebloom. They have been hyper-distracted and crazy-busy since we arrived, doing out-of-character and mind-bendingly ordinary things like applying for jobs that involve zero travel, signing up at the doctor's, and shoe-horning us into schools. These are not activities we are used to our parents being busy at. In fact, they are the total opposite of what we have spent our whole lives being taught to expect. It is very unsettling. Claude reckons Mum and Dad had radical personality transplants, like, overnight, when we weren't looking. She says they might not actually be our original parents any more, and we need to stay alert, because absolutely anything could be about to happen.

I say, 'Are you sure they're the only ones?' because right now I would bet money on the fact she's had the personality transplant too. She definitely isn't acting like my original sister. She isn't nearly as much fun as she used to be.

I haven't had anything transplanted. I am exactly the same as ever, even though everything else has changed. My name can't be shortened and I don't have a middle one. It is what it is, and everyone just calls me Joy.

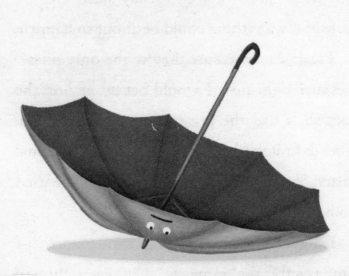

2

The here that we have got to is Grandad's house.

His name is Thomas Blake, and he is Mum's dad, although sometimes I find it hard to believe they are even related. I would never *ever* pick them out of a line-up of fathers and daughters, unless I knew. Not in a million. Grandad is sort of faint and blurry, like someone drew him with a soft pencil, and Mum is marker-pen dark. Mum is loud and bombastic and colourful, and Grandad is more narrow and faded and quiet. Mum is a socialist, which is a long political word for being good-at-sharing, and Grandad? Well, Grandad is not. Mum says we are world citizens and should support the free movement of people across the globe, and I think Grandad would prefer to put a nice tall fence around this one little island, and cover it in great big signs that say,

NO TRESPASSING

and

PRIVATE PROPERTY

and

KEEP OUT.

Our family does not see eye to eye with Grandad on a long list of things. I think that's why we spend so much time talking to him about the weather.

The letters on his doormat say Mr T. E. Blake but he won't tell me what the E is for, so I have decided to guess. I have been allowing myself a new guess every day. I don't think I am close to getting it right, but so far he has not decided to correct me, so I'm just going to carry on trying.

Thomas Elephant Blake's face is full of pockets and pouches like a backpack and when he speaks, the pockets and pouches fill and empty with air. The letters he gets are mostly catalogues for slippers that plug into the wall, and baths with actual doors in the side for getting in and out, and hearing aids disguised as reading glasses. I think the catalogues are brilliant and inventive, but Thomas Eggcup Blake does not agree. He says that having permanently cold feet and not being able to climb in and out of the bath or hear and see properly are not reasons to celebrate. I think he says that about a lot of things. I'm not sure he is really the celebrating kind. He is mostly grey from head to toe, like he has just walked through a room where the ceiling fell in. Claude says that wouldn't happen at Thomas Eagle-Eye Blake's house, where everything looks scared of being out of place. She says the ceilings wouldn't be brave enough. They actually wouldn't dare.

Mum is keen for us all to get along like a house on fire, another thing my sister says would never happen, seeing as Grandad goes around at night switching every single plug socket off. We aren't supposed to make up our minds about him yet, because we don't know him well enough to reach a proper verdict. Mum says, Family is Family is Family, whatever side of the fence you're on, whatever your domestic habits or whatever you believe. Dad says we all need to be patient with each other, and spend more time together, and let the dust settle.

Claude says, 'Fat chance,' and I think, 'What dust? There isn't even one speck,' but they both say that it will be worth the wait, and that eventually the real Grandad will emerge like a butterfly coming out of its chrysalis, or at least a snake shedding its old skin.

I have seen thousands and thousands of Monarch butterflies hatching in Mexico, turning the hillsides a living, quivering red, and I have watched a rattlesnake leave behind its own skin outside in the hot sand, quick and papery as a crayon wrapper. So I wonder exactly how soon and how spectacular Thomas Extravaganza Blake's big reveal might actually be.

Claude shakes her head at me, and then at Mum and Dad, and then at our new squashed-in world in general, and says something muffled and full of gravel about nobody bothering to hold their breath.

3

Before we landed here, we had always travelled about. A lot. The four of us have been moving and living and working and mucking about in all sorts of parts of the world since I was a baby, since before I can even remember. Claude and Mum and Dad and me. We have always been free as birds. Claude keeps a list somewhere, in one of her many notebooks, of all the different places we have been, and I've forgotten the exact number, but there are 195 countries in the world and counting, so we were only just getting started.

Grandad likes to call what we did 'gallivanting about the globe'. Mum and Dad always called it 'living'.

Before, if we were a family of plants, we would have been sycamore blades or maple keys or those bits of dandelion fluff that float along on the breeze from one place to another, minding their own business, going places, never worrying where.

Mum used to watch the sunset over wherever we were, and sigh in a good way and say, 'Aren't we lucky?' She used to say she could never see us stuck in one place, in a box, on a street with identical boxes, all nailed down.

And the rest of us agreed.

When it was hard to leave stuff behind, there were always new things ahead of us to make up for it. The giggling sisters in the café in Hanoi that makes the sweet soup, or the elephant boats in Mumbai, or Fabiola, the girl in Mexico City who taught me Spanish at the exact same time as teaching me how to roller-skate, so that I didn't even realize until later that I was learning to do both.

And if problems started to mount up, such as giant mosquito bites, or genuine real-life cooked guinea pigs on the menu, or traffic fumes as thick and damp as cotton wool, then moving day was a very handy thing that could not come fast enough.

So far, I have grown up always looking forward to what's next. For as long as I can remember, there has been something interesting to do and somewhere exciting to be right around the corner.

The four of us have liked it that way, and I've never known anything else, which is why Mum and Dad say it's no surprise that I'm the sunniest, most adventurous person they know.

When Mum and Dad told us about moving back here, we were 7,403km away in Zanzibar, an island in the Indian Ocean off the coast of Tanzania, on the east coast of Africa. Mum was working at a hospital, and Dad did lessons with us most mornings, and shifts in the kitchen of a hotel. Mum is a nurse and Dad is a chef. He is hands down the best cook I know. His food puts a smile even on Claude's face, sometimes even now. I'm sure that Mum is good at her job too, but she is not even in the same league as Dad when it comes to cooking.

In Zanzibar we lived in a concrete house with nets over the windows and at night I fell asleep looking at the holes in the nets, full of sky, and listening to the in-and-out breathing of the sea. The tide at our favourite beach went out so far that we had to walk over a kilometre to get to the edge of the water. The sand was damp and fine and silvery white, and the sun cut out our shadows with scissors, and the ocean and the sky were the same bright, vivid gemstone blue.

There are coral reefs around the edges of Zanzibar, like a living breathing wall. On just an ordinary average afternoon, we'd see turtles and seahorses and frog fish and trumpet fish and anemone crabs and stone fish and more than one octopus, just by being there, without even trying. They didn't take any notice of us, just went about their quick-slow, underwater business, while over their heads we made great big storm clouds in their sky. The sun broke into patterns beneath the surface of the ocean and we swam through patchworks of warm and then cold, and there was a whole world down there, full of shadows and light.

It was 1st April and we were playing football with Joseph and Godfrey and Prosper. Joseph and Prosper are brothers, and Godfrey's dad worked at the same hospital as Mum. For weeks we had been making a ball out of plastic bags. Every time we found a new one we added it. Prosper showed us how to, because he'd done it a million times before. You have to wrap it properly and be very precise, or it goes all loose and baggy and the ball won't work because it won't be a ball at all, just a big lump of bag. When Prosper grows up, he is going to make his fortune building clever things out of all the stuff other people throw away. Plastics are worse than a nuisance on the island, and tourists are banned from bringing them and then leaving them lying around, but it happens anyway. That ball was just about reaching maximum size for any game, and the boys were already talking about what we were going to make next, which was a kind of kayak made from bottles. I was really looking forward to that, but we left before the first bottle-kayak was even finished. Sometimes, I picture them all paddling through the gemstone waves on the other side of the world. I bet Prosper made a special rudder for his, maybe out of an aerial and some bits of flipper, so he could control the direction of travel. I picture the turtles and seahorses and frog fish and trumpet fish and anemone crabs and stone fish and more than one octopus, all ignoring them as they go splashing and laughing by.

Moving day has never been a big deal for us because we are so used to it. There is always something else around the corner and somewhere new to go. But when Claude and I got home on 1st April, we couldn't miss the red flags.

For a start, Mum and Dad were both there. In Zanzibar, they were only ever home at the same time on Friday evenings, and this was a Wednesday. Red Flag Number One.

Also, they had been pacing up and down and waiting for us to get home, we could tell. Very unusual. Red Flag Number Two.

Red Flag Number Three, the great big elephant in the room one, was Dad saying, 'Crisps or biscuits?'

I can't explain how extremely, eye-wateringly out of character this question was. The start of his personality transplant, right there. Our dad thinks crisps are the food of the devil. He can talk for a bewilderingly long time about just how devilish they are. When he does it, literally all Claude and I can think about is crisps.

'Crisps,' we both said, at the same time, and we looked at each other.

Claude can do that thing with her eyebrow, so one goes up and the other one stays where it is, which, if you ask me, is about the best way in the world to say, 'Wait, what?' without actually speaking. I can't do the eyebrow thing but I can roll my tongue into a sort of Swiss roll, and she can't, so that makes us even, except that rolling your tongue isn't a good or quick way to send any kind of message. According to Claude, the difference between us has got everything to do with genetics and nothing to do with actual skills.

'What's the surprise?' I said, and Claude said, 'What's wrong?'

'Sit down,' said Mr and Mrs Red Flag, so we did, and Claude did the eyebrow thing again, and I Swiss-rolled my tongue back and forth.

Our replacement parents breathed in, quite loudly, both at the same time, and for a minute none of us said anything. Not a word. I opened my crisps. Cheese and onion. The only noise in the room was the crunching, like boots on gravel, louder in my ears than the tide-out, half-distant sound of the waves. For half a minute, I wondered if those crisps were as loud for everyone else as they were for me.

'Claude,' I said, with my mouth kind of wedged open and one big crisp stuck halfway in.

She was staring at her packet like it was a bad thing wrapped inside a good thing, a gift with a terrible price tag attached. 'What?'

'Open yours,' I said, and she did.

Mum and Dad were super-serious. They looked like they'd lost something instead of winning it. Red Flag Number Four.

'We're leaving,' Dad said, not at all in the way he would normally say it.

'Where are we going?' I said.

'Home,' Mum said.

Claude said, 'Huh?' and I said, 'Where's

that?' at the exact same time.

'Britain,' said Dad. 'You know. The UK.'

Claude did the eyebrow thing again. 'Who died?' she said, and Mum's face went dark like a shadow, like something high up just flew right over her head.

'No one.'

'The *UK*?' Claude said, like an echo.

Mum and Dad nodded. 'Yep.'

'But that's not home. You hate it there,' Claude said, and Mum's nod changed to a sort of side to side, like a maybe. 'Well, that's not strictly true.'

'Yes, it is,' Claude said. 'We haven't lived there for ten years,' and then she pointed at me. 'Joy's *never* lived there,' and I felt my face go hot, and my stomach beginning to buzz.

I was a hive of questions. Everything I could

think of to say started with what or how or where or when or why? I thought if I opened my mouth bees might fly out.

'Is this a joke?' Claude said. 'It is, isn't it? Good one. April Fool. You got us.'

Mum and Dad didn't laugh or even smile. Red Flag Number Five.

Claude said, 'Really? Truthfully?'

Home. It wasn't something I'd really thought of before. It had never been an actual place on the map. It was just wherever Mum and Dad and Claude were.

I asked when this move might be happening. I explained that the sea-turtle sanctuary was planning a release into the wild pretty soon, and it only happened once a year, and the date had been fixed in my mind for weeks. I was crossing my fingers behind my back because I really wanted to be around for that. I volunteered at the turtle sanctuary on Tuesday afternoons, which according to Claude meant that I followed people around and got under their feet, but actually means I got to help feed wounded turtles and clean out their tanks and hose down stuff and wear a special staff T-shirt and be a very valuable member of the team. Turtle Tuesday was my favourite day of the week in Zanzibar.

Dad scratched at his chin, same as he did when he was re-learning long division so that he could teach it to us. He walked across the room and looked at the calendar, and then he smiled in a weak, watery daylight kind of way.

'I think you might just make it, Joy.'

'Really?' Mum said, and he nodded.

My whole head filled with relief, like a sea mist. 'Oh, GOOD.'

'Why does this feel *off*?' Claude was saying. 'What's the big hurry?'

'It's time,' Dad said, and Claude said, 'But why?'

Mum looked at Dad and he looked at us. 'Because of Grandad.'

'Grandad?' I said, and the word felt weird in my mouth, because I hadn't ever used it all that much.

Mum closed her eyes and started wiping them with her sleeve. And that was it. The difference. The reason we were moving this time. Not for a new job or a piece of research or a famous mountain range or a breathtaking landscape. Not for curiosity or adventure or a bit of a change. Not just for a because.

We were coming home for Thomas Emergency Blake.

4

While I was snorkelling in the Indian Ocean with Claude, and Mum was running her Wednesday vaccination clinic, and Dad was getting ready to make a crayfish salad special, Thomas Everest Blake was climbing a ladder to change the light bulb on his kitchen ceiling. Then he was falling and banging his head hard enough to make him pass out, and breaking his hip and his right arm in two places, the wrist and the elbow.

When he woke up, it took him a long time to get to his phone. It took him a long time to remember his address and a long time for the ambulance to reach him. It took the longest of all the times for us to find out 7,403km away what had happened. I think he fell off the ladder nearly two days before Mum and Dad knew about it.

Mum said, 'Nobody is going through that again.'

Claude and I looked at each other. Suddenly everything made sense, even the crisps, because we both knew exactly what she was talking about.

Our Granny Hester, Grandad's wife, Mum's mum, died suddenly, six years ago, when I was four and we were 8,576km away in the Cloud Forest in Costa Rica.

That part of the forest is extremely remote. It doesn't have anything even close to WiFi or a phone signal, and I'm guessing that's exactly why we went there. That's also exactly why we didn't hear the news about Hester for more than a week.

According to Mum, there are things in life that cut through time like a knife, so there will always and forever be a Before, with a capital B, and also an After, when everything has changed. Granny Hester dying so unexpectedly, and also being dead for so long before she even found out, is extremely and definitely one of those things. And when Grandad fell and hurt himself all on his own, Mum thought it might be the start of another.

I suppose Grandad falling from a ladder

and us coming back from Zanzibar are perfect examples of actions having consequences, of cause and effect.

I sat on the sofa eating crisps and watching the hot beach outside our shady concrete house and I thought about Thomas Explorer Blake deciding to change that bulb, and losing his balance. And then on his way down, all the things he must have thought about, all the things that must have raced through his mind.

We have spent a lot of time in places where older people are cared for and respected at the heart of the family. Mum was saying, 'How could I live with myself if I didn't take good care of my own dad?'

'Can he come out here?' Claude said. 'And be with us where we are? In the heart of *this* family?'

'Not in his condition,' said Dad. 'He's got three broken bones and a concussion.'

'Well, later, then?' Claude said.

'Yes,' I said. 'When he's better, he could come on a trip with us. I think he might like Mombasa!'

I was looking forward to it even before I'd finished saying it. Who wouldn't love Mombasa?

'Couldn't *you* go and look after him,' Claude was saying to Mum, 'and leave us where we are, and then bring him out when you come back?'

Mum didn't look too hopeful.

'It's not a quick fix,' she said. 'There's more to it than that.'

'Like what?'

'He's very . . . settled, my dad,' she said,

looking at the floor and at her own fingernails, looking anywhere except at us. 'He might not want to leave home, where all his memories are.'

'He can make new memories,' I said, while Claude screwed up her empty crisp packet and aimed it at the recycling. She missed, and blew all her mouth air out into her cheeks.

'Well, this just gets more fun every minute I think about it,' she said.

'Not everything is about having fun, Claude,' said Dad.

Right then, I knew it was serious. I knew we couldn't in a million years have Thomas Elderly Blake being lonely and sad and breaking hips and arms just from trying to change a light bulb. And we couldn't have Mum feeling guilty and ashamed either. So we had to find things to be happy about. *Home*, if that's what the UK was going to be, had famous cities, and lush green countryside, and the River Thames, and the National Health Service and dogs as pets and the RSPCA. I have only been there once, after Granny Hester died, and I always wanted to look out over the whole of London on the big Eye, and maybe visit the Jurassic Coast, with its fossils that started off in the centre of the planet and ended up somewhere near Exeter. And Stonehenge and the Eden Project and the Isle of Skye. *Home* had family in it. A Grandad we didn't even properly know yet. Those were enough good things to be getting on with.

That April Fool's night in Zanzibar, I lay in bed listening to the sea breathing in and out and I thought about moving again, and how new and silvery it was all going to turn out to be. I wondered about so many different things. Like what the UK smelled like. And what my favourite thing to eat would be. And how much weather there was actually. And what it would be like to speak and hear everywhere in English.

I wondered too what I'd be able to hear from my bed at Thomas England Blake's house.

Now here we are. And 'Traffic' is the answer to that question. And at certain times of night, if I lie on my side and put my pillow over my ear, the cars coming and going past the end of the road sound almost like slow night-time waves, and if I try hard enough I can fall asleep pretending that I'm still somewhere else, in a house that has soft netting over the windows, with the moon making a pathway across the jet-black shimmering sea.

5

Thomas Earthling Blake's house is in a street called Plane Tree Gardens, which I would call imaginative and Claude says is a blatant, open-and-shut case of false advertising. We haven't seen one plane tree, not anywhere, and the gardens are about the size of envelopes, and all paved over, and full of enormous bins.

I was looking forward to a street full of plane trees. They have flaky bark and big round seed clumps like a tennis ball and they are really tall and easy to climb because of the way they spread their branches like an octopus with open arms. I'm quite good at climbing trees and I have been high up in quite a few.

The houses in Plane Tree-less Gardens don't have personalities of their own. They are identical, which makes them impossible to tell apart. This is a problem when you are coming home from the park and can't remember which house you're living in. They all have exactly the same low black metal gates and stingy little windows and thundercloud grey front doors. I have daydreamed about going out in the middle of the night with some spray cans and painting those doors bright new colours until there is no more thundercloud grey in sight, apart from in the actual sky. But at the moment, the only difference I can find between the houses is the numbers. Now I have committed it to memory, I can say with total confidence that this one is number 48.

The people here don't seem to do much talking to each other. Everyone keeps their head down and their eyes looking the other way, and nobody is what I would call welcoming, not so far anyway, especially when you are mistakenly but perfectly innocently trying to let yourself into their house. But I am working on making friends, in my own way. I have one or two plans up my sleeve that might involve free cupcakes, home-made lemonade, a neighbourhood book swap and a food-of-the-world day, if I'm ever allowed.

Claude says, 'You don't live in a children's book from the 1970s, you know,' and I say, 'No, I live in boring old Plane Tree Gardens, and I am trying to make the best of it.'

Thomas Earwax Blake doesn't know his neighbours' real names, even though they have all been living here for longer than I've been able to ride a bike. The ones on the left he calls the Shouters and the ones on the right he calls Messy. Claude wonders under her breath what names they might have for him. I pretend I don't hear her saying that.

Mum and Dad shake their heads and say that this street and this town and this country have changed a lot in the ten years that they have been gone. They also shake their heads and say that 48 Plane Tree Gardens has not. Then they look straight at me.

'Come on, Joy,' Dad says, and Mum says, 'You can find the silver lining on any cloud.'

I look outside at the low drizzle. I know the sun is up there somewhere, shining away, even if I can't actually see it. 'Okay then,' I tell them. 'I'll do my best.'

On the inside, the house is mostly brown and yellow, with the odd pop of green that reminds me of a mossy forest. Claude calls the colour scheme *things that have gone off in the fridge*. The furniture is moody and dark, with handles that rattle at you when you walk past, as if they are trying to tell you something. The flowers on the sitting-room curtains are big and squashed, like they've been trodden on by a herd of cows in the rain. The brown-and-yellow lino on the kitchen floor looks new in some places, and worn almost to nothing where Grandad has spent forty years treading – at the sink, next to the cooker and right by the back door. There are extremely breakable china ornaments everywhere of frowning dogs and cats and old-fashioned people who look like they were turned to stone in the middle of a particularly boring conversation. Mum says it's all exactly the same as it was when she was growing up, and Claude says, 'Well, no wonder you left and didn't want to come back, then.'

Mum hasn't really got an answer for that.

We have always been very good at sharing small spaces. We have curled up together in tents and on trains and in cabins and it has been better than fine. We have lived together in smaller places, much smaller, so I'm still trying to work out why 48 Plane

Tree Gardens feels like an all-day game of Sardines without enough of the actual fun. Grandad has his own bedroom, of course, same as always. Claude and I share the other one, and Mum and Dad sleep downstairs on the sofa, which is making them look about as crumpled in the mornings as their sheets. Everybody seems to want to use the bathroom and the kettle and the hot water and the toaster and the landline at the same time. There is always someone in the one doorway you need to go through, or someone else you have to stop for, halfway down the stairs. There are chairs you can and can't sit on, things you must and mustn't touch. We crowd around the same objects like they are the sugar and we are the ants.

Claude says we are in Thomas Emperor

Blake's way, and that he is used to having the whole place to himself. She thinks this is the definition of ironic, seeing as if it was up to her, he could have it all back and just keep it. According to my sister, Grandad's empire is a dump. It hasn't got one thing to recommend it, and no distinguishing features whatsoever. She says her review would give it zero stars for everything, and she wouldn't even send her worst enemy here. I'm not sure who her worst enemy is at the moment: maybe Mum or Dad, for bringing us here in the first place. When I try to ask, she glares at me like I am another huge waste of her extremely precious time, and I worry, for half a second or so, that her worst enemy might, in actual fact, be me.

Claude has asked our parents about

eighty-nine times how long they think we will be staying here. A year, according to Mum, but Dad says it's more like two, and both of their faces say that they actually have no clue.

'Here?' Claude says. 'In this house?' and they say, 'For the time being. We all just need to find our feet.'

Claude groans like a howler monkey and says it already feels like forever. She stretches the word out agonizingly slowly, so it takes its own personal forever to happen. I put my hands over my ears and remember some of the times we have found our feet in other places, like the hot red dust of Jaipur, or the ice-cold water of a Swiss mountain stream, or a noisy street corner in New York City, looking up at all the buildings and the little squares of sky while our heartbeats quicken. I remind myself that we know how to do this, and it is all just a matter of time.

6

I have only ever been here in the UK once before, ages ago. That was for one week, and this, like Claude says, is more like for-ev-er.

All I really remember from my one visit is that the rain didn't stop, hardly at all, apart from the day we visited Grandma Hester's grave, when the sun suddenly shone blindingly bright and the ground crunched with frost and the sky was hard and flat, like steel. Everything I touched that day was cold, including Claude's fingers which went numb and waxy like candles until we were sure they were about to drop off. I also remember that Mum cried and cried and said 'I can't believe I missed my mother's funeral.'

And now here we are again, in this house and this town and this country, this smallest atom on the head of a pin stuck in the world map. And like Claude says, storybook magic isn't going to save us any time soon. We are cold again too, all the time, and it's dull like someone turned the lights and the colour down. We don't know anyone outside of our own family, and we can't make friends out of thin air, because nobody has the book with that spell in it. All the rules have changed, almost overnight, and they seem to be numberless, and we are constantly being told what to do in new, surprising and short-tempered ways.

In our old life, we were very adaptable. Routines changed depending on where we were and what we were up to. Sometimes we woke up at dawn, before the birds, and cooked breakfast outside on a fire while every creature around us was still pressing snooze. Sometimes we lounged around in our pyjamas with the TV on extra loud. Sometimes, we stayed up all night to watch the Northern Lights dance their cliff-drop-silent way across the sky, and sometimes we trekked for days through the rainforest, all soaked and breathless and too tired even to stop and eat.

It's hard to stick to the same old rules in so many new places. There really isn't any point. We got so used to our days being full of surprises, that even when we thought we knew what was going to happen, we also knew that something different was bound to show up in its place. That was almost the only thing that was reliable – that nothing was.

But I guess you don't realize that the way you do things is unusual or different until you find yourself face to face with someone else's definition of normal. Now our normal has collided with Grandad's, and we are all doing our best to make it work.

Thomas Efficiency Blake would love Japanese public transport with all of his highly organized heart. He gets up every single morning at six, like clockwork. Not five or seven or ten minutes past. Six o'clock on the dot. I know this because I have checked. At 6.03 a.m., he goes downstairs in his dressing gown and slippers and puts the kettle on, and then he feeds the cat, who is quite snooty actually, and not interested in making friends with me for a start, and is called Buster. Buster never gets fed first, before the kettle goes on, because in Grandad's world that would be chaos. After he has made himself a cup of tea (brewed in a pot, while he counts to one hundred) he lets Buster out and then stands at the window for six to eight minutes, drinking and watching the cat's bum fashion-show itself leisurely down the path. He uses the bathroom from 6.15 a.m. until 6.30 a.m. sharp, and when he comes out he is fully dressed and his hair is combed down with something that makes it look a bit like grey plastic. After that, he doesn't really have any pressing or urgent business until 9.30 p.m., which is without fail when he goes to bed and expects the rest of us to do the same. His shoes are so shiny with polish you can see your face in them. His coat buttons are always done up. He never loses a glove or steps in a puddle or forgets his wallet. He is always where he says he is going to be, without fail, almost to the minute, exactly on time.

I don't know how he does it. Claude says he is half man half stopwatch, with whirring dials and hands and cogs just under his skin, like a futuristic robot in a very old-fashioned film. She says it is the only explanation she can find for so much mind-bending punctuality.

If me and Claude and Mum and Dad were in charge of timetables, trains would go to surprise destinations, and leave early, or take three extra days, or decide not to leave at all. There would be hundreds and hundreds of complaints. Grandad says we are very *free range* but he doesn't say it in a good way, like you would about chickens. He thinks the four of us are about as organized as a bag of wild cats and about as relaxing as a spot of white-water rafting, and Dad says he is probably right.

Claude says being organized is overrated, and that she likes white-water rafting a whole lot more than she likes watching puddles through the kitchen window on a dreary afternoon, while the clock on the wall ticks her life away.

'I don't care how accurate it is,' she says. 'It's still an hour and a half I'm never going to get back.'

In Grandad's normal there are maximum speeds of moving, and limits on noise levels and right and wrong ways of doing household chores. There are places to put (and absolutely not put) our shoes and coats and keys and the recycling and Claude's books and my art box. There are even rules against singing, and I know because I broke them on Day One. In fact, I have broken most of Grandad's rules since I got here, by accident, mainly because I didn't know about them and I can't keep track. 48 Plane Tree Gardens is a Niagara Falls of manners and we are in a barrel like Houdini, always going over the edge.

I must admit, it is not what I was hoping for. Not yet. Not what I was expecting at all.

It feels like a full stop, when all we have ever been used to is commas.

Claude says nothing is certain any more. But this is what I know:

I miss the light of other places, and the colour.

I miss slices of fresh starfruit and sweet potato, with chilli and lime, cooked on a fire in a barrel on the side of the road and wrapped in a scrap of newspaper, too hot to touch.

I miss watching other people's worlds go by through a grubby train window, non-stop, like TV, with the sound of the rails.

I miss the feeling of being in a crowd, on a bus, or at a market maybe, or a station, and not understanding a single word that anyone is saying, so that they might as well all be birds to me, calling out to each other in a forest, just letting me be there, and not minding at all.

We aren't seeds on the breeze any more. We are a thing with roots and foundations, something stuck in the ground like a motorway bridge, or a lamp post, or a tree.

We are birds in captivity now, which is the

opposite of free. And nobody is finding it easy.

I also know that out there somewhere, is some everyday, real-life magic that can help us. Even this normal has a silver lining, because everything does. And I'm sure that I will find it. I just have to keep my head up and keep looking. I am hatching and scheming and plotting, or trying to anyway. And it's a good thing I'm bothering, because the rest of them, Mum and Dad and Claude and even Grandad, seem to be looking at me expectantly, like my official family job title is Problem Solver, and they have paid me in advance, and it's all down to me to deliver.

7

When I met Prosper and Joseph and Godfrey in Zanzibar, we played a lot of games, like Charades and Kick the Can and Twenty Questions and Losey Friendy. I made up songs and put on plays and baked sticky sweets with my friend Rupi in Mumbai. A boy called Brad let me draw on the pavement outside his house in New York with these really big chalks. When I meet someone for the first time, as well as doing stuff, I want to find out everything I can, like what their favourite animal is, and what they most like to eat for breakfast and what they would take with them if they went on a last-minute trip to the moon. I have loads more good questions like that up my sleeve. Meeting new people is the best thing about starting again in another place.

It occurs to me that Grandad is a nearly new person, even though he is old, and we are related. And 48 Plane Tree Gardens is a nearly new place, even if I have been here once before. So I have decided to ask questions and plan fun stuff and get him to play some games with me. I am going to do what I always do, everywhere, and start making friends.

Thomas Earthling Blake's favourite animal is an otter. He eats porridge for breakfast. Every day. And for some unknown reason he puts salt in it instead of sugar. He has no idea what he would take to the moon at short notice, and no idea why I asked. He doesn't seem very keen on the thought of baking or drawing on the pavement, probably because of the mess. He looks flustered when I want to know if he has any packs of cards tucked away somewhere. He has never heard of Kick the Can and he says it sounds like a waste of time.

It is a good job I am working hard at this, because something is already telling me that Grandad is going to be a very tough nut to crack.

At dinner time, we are all squeezed round the table with our elbows tucked in and our eyes down and our mouths very much closed for chewing. There is not quite enough talking and there is not nearly enough room. I feel like a giant in a doll's house and I'm easily the smallest one there. Claude's eye-rolling is off the charts. I figure if I don't do something good very soon, then something bad is bound to happen.

So I take a deep breath, and I count to three inside my own head, and then I start with the Alphabet game. Everybody apart from Grandad knows the rules.

'You make up stories together,' I tell him. 'With words that have to begin with the letters, in the right order, from A to Z.'

I also tell him he can go last.

'You'll pick it up,' I say. 'It's easy,' and before he can ask any more questions or find a reason not to play, I get started.

'*Always,*' I say, and Claude sighs loudly, like

this is the last thing she wants to be doing.

'*Bring,*' she says.

Dad says, '*Colourful*' and Mum says, '*Dogs*', and then we count to five and wait for Grandad to think.

'*Everywhere?*' he says, and I clap my hands and jiggle around a bit in my seat with delight that he is even trying.

Grandad frowns, and then I say, '*For*' and Claude says, '*Great*' in her bored-est voice and Dad says, '*Holidays*' and Mum says, '*In*' and we wait again, not for so long this time.

Grandad says, '*July?*' and I clap again and grin at him and try my very best to sit still.

After '*Kim likes mainly non-organic parsnips*' and '*Red squirrels tremble under volcanoes*' and '*We X-rayed Yussuf's Zebra*', Claude has had enough.

She is very good at drawing, so I suggest we play a game of Consequences. I start trying to tell Grandad about how you make a weird creature by drawing a bit and then folding your piece of paper over and passing it on to the next person. Halfway through my explanation, Claude puts her hand out to stop me. She counts on her fingers, pointing to each of us in turn, including herself.

'Head,' she says. 'Chest with arms, stomach, legs, feet.'

I keep my smile under wraps because it will annoy her if I draw attention to the fact that she is actually joining in. I draw the head of a bottle-nosed dolphin and then I fold it very carefully so only a tiny bit is showing, and I pass it on.

When we open it up for the big reveal, Mum

has drawn the chest and arms of Mr Tickle and Dad has done the stomach of a beetle and Claude has drawn beautiful ballet dancer legs and Grandad has done enormous scuba-diver flippers. It is our dream-creature from the deep. 'Our first piece of art,' I say, and I get up and stick it on the fridge with a thing that looks like a raindrop. Grandad only seems to have magnets that are signs for bad weather. Mind you, I am surprised he has any fridge magnets at all. He looks a bit uncomfortable that I have used them to stick anything anywhere.

After Consequences, I switch to the New Name game. This is one of my all-time favourites, because it's extremely silly and lets everyone become somebody who is miles away from who they actually are. In the New Name game, you get to choose yourself, and what you do for a job, and how you speak and walk and all sorts of other little things that turn you into another person. It is different every single time. You don't need any equipment. All you have to do is talk without thinking, and say the first thing that pops into your head. One minute you can be Warburton Smythe, store detective, with fourteen cats, a handlebar moustache and a bossy aunt who only ever wears purple, and the next you can be Tamara Hatbox, ballroom dancer and jewel thief, on the run from the police and violently allergic to clams. It is amazing what people choose. And it's funny how well you get to know somebody when they are pretending to be someone else.

Claude doesn't want to play the New Name game. She leaves the table and slouches over to a tired saggy armchair. 'I'm not in the right mood,' she says. 'I can't think of anyone to be.'

This is the rubbish-est excuse for not playing I have ever heard. I give her two suggestions off the top of my head, that's how easy this game is.

'Be Jeffrey Winter, the willow-weaving trapeze artist who makes his own costumes from leaves,' I tell her, and Claude shakes her head.

'Be Peanut Banks, the long-distance runner with hair down to her knees and a voice like sandpaper,' I say, and Claude gives me one of her blankest, most deadliest looks.

'NO.'

Her nose is scrunched up like she can smell something quite nasty nearby and she scowls at the ornaments on the shelf like she is thinking about knocking them down.

There is a minute when nobody says anything, and I wonder if Claude has just managed to handbrake all the fun before I could even get it really started. I look at her and pull a face, which is supposed to make her laugh, but doesn't.

'What are you even *doing*?' she says.

'Having FUN,' I tell her. 'Come on. Come back.'

'I'm good over here, thanks,' she says, even though anyone who is looking can see that she is not.

'Well, what *do* you want to play, then?' I ask her.

Claude blows all the air out through her mouth. 'How about a game of *Shut Up and Leave Me Alone*?'

'How do you play that?' Grandad says, and

my face goes a bit hot and Mum and Dad have to explain that there is no such thing.

Grandad isn't sure he understands the rules to the New Name game, probably because there aren't any. But he still manages to turn himself into Hyacinth Von Ramen, noodle heiress and synchronised swimming champion, within about half a minute of starting to play. He is actually a natural. He makes his voice all wobbly and high, and pinches his nose tight shut like he is underwater. Hyacinth makes me laugh until I am crying. And then I know for a fact that even though things are a bit difficult and strange, and some people (like Claude) are being grumpy and rude, and other people (like Mum and Dad) are being very serious, there is still good news, peeking through the clouds like a flash of sunshine on a wet, grey day. And that good news is that Grandad and I are going to get along fine.

Then, just when we are starting to make friends, Thomas Exit Blake looks at the clock and screws up his eyes and yawns.

'That's more than enough action in one day for me,' he says.

'Really?' I ask him, because I thought we were just getting started. 'Are you sure?'

He looks at me, and blinks. 'It has been a *bewildering* evening.'

I am hoping that is a good thing. Grandad stands up and pushes his chair in, so it is neat and in a straight line, just like everything else. He pulls at his cardigan to get the creases out and he looks down at the reflection of the light bulb in his shoes. He isn't smiling. He looks very thoughtful and serious. I am crossing my fingers behind my back that he has liked our first try at friend-making activities, because I can't help already thinking of lots more.

Grandad coughs a little bit, to clear his throat. He goes to the stairs without a word and then he stops and comes back again, just so his head and shoulders are in the doorway of the room, like the first bit of a game of Consequences.

'Do you know,' he says. 'I don't think I've had that much fun in years.'

Claude is still grumpy when we go to bed. But I'm not. I'm still smiling, and there is a pattering, like very light rain or the bubbles in lemonade, gently popping in my chest, because I have a really good feeling – my new-place feeling – about what's coming next, and what might be waiting for us, just around the corner.

8

The next day, I am begging Claude for about the four millionth time to get off her bum and come outside and do something with me, when Grandad says, 'Things will be better when you start school.'

And there it is. The news I have been waiting for. Something BIG. Something I can be ready for, and try hard at, and get my teeth into.

'Really? Honestly?' I have to stop myself

from jumping up and down on the spot. 'School? When?'

I have been curious for ages about what a real-life actual school might be like. I am picturing rooms filled with books and paints, and endless things to make and do, and busy playgrounds swimming with kids, like shoals of fishes. I am imagining making so many new friends that I can't even count them. I am thinking about school trips and school plays and school clubs and school fairs. Ideas are pinging about in my head like grasshoppers.

So I am surprised when Claude says the word, 'School?' because she says it very differently to me.

'*School?*' she says again, and her eyes get bigger.

I stop pinging, and Mum and Dad give each

other a look that says, 'Uh oh. Here we go.'

'Well,' Thomas Education Blake says, wading blindly into enemy territory, carrying on regardless. 'It will get you both out of the house.'

My sister raises her eyebrows, both at the same time. 'Oh no. No. *No*. NO,' she says, and the fear in her voice makes my neck go stiff and my legs start to tingle as if they are about to melt. The only other time this has happened was when I was looking down into the Grand Canyon. It's the feeling of falling, like someone just whipped the floor out from underneath you, and seeing just how far away the bottom is.

This is Claude's big nightmare – the total opposite of the icing on the cake, and I am watching her struggle with how exactly to react. Grandad has just chucked it out there, like cooked pasta at a wall, to see if it sticks, and it has stuck to my sister in a big way. Her eyes are like plates, and she looks from Mum to Dad and back again, and then she says, 'Are you seriously doing this to us?'

Mum and Dad nod, and squeeze out a 'Yes' and then Claude just keeps saying, 'Why? WhyWhyWhyWhyWhy?' like it's the only word in her head, flying round and round in circles like a bat, getting its bearings in the dark of her skull.

School was never part of our old normal, and Claude always liked it that way. Mum and (mostly) Dad taught us stuff in clever and ingenious ways, on the move and sometimes so we didn't realize we were even learning until the lesson was done. Never going to school has taught me and Claude all sorts of things. We can speak three and a half languages, and we know some good swear words in five or six more. We know how to find our way using the sky, even without a compass, and we know how to read maps and sail a small boat and filter water and spot poisonous snakes and bugs and plants without too much trouble. We are good swimmers and fast runners and excellent roller-skaters. We can write pretty good stories and Claude can draw brilliant cartoons and make three different kinds of bread and I can name all the planets and quite a few stars. We understand latitude and longitude and altitude. And magnets and Celsius and velocity and momentum. We know the periodic table off by heart because of a song. We have heard of Shakespeare and the Brontë sisters, and Mahatma Gandhi and Maya Angelou and Albert Einstein and Marie Curie and Nelson Mandela and Alexander Fleming and Aesop and Malala Yousafzai and Guru Nanak and Katherine Johnson and Alan Turing and Lewis Carroll and Mary Seacole and Greta Thunberg and Scheherazade and Anansi the Spider and Hanuman and Rama and the Incomparable Mulla Nasrudin. We have tried very hard to be good at trigonometry and we are both not that bad at playing the ukulele and the violin, even though there is nowhere in Plane Tree Gardens to practise that doesn't end up with someone whose middle name begins with 'E' coming into the room with his hands over his ears and begging you to stop.

'Whyyyy?' Claude says again, one more

time, like she's in some kind of trance, with the bat still circling her brain, using its ears for eyes.

Mum explains that she and Dad both have to get full-time jobs, for financial reasons. She says there won't be enough hours in the day to home school us like they used to. Dad says something about everyone dealing with changes and new experiences, and stepping into unknowns, and it being the right time. Claude does a sock-puppet thing with her hands, like *blah blah blah* and then rolls her eyes into the back of her head and lies down flat on the living-room floor like she has died, refusing to move, so that everyone has to step over her like she's an anthill or a bump in the road. Thomas Eyeball Blake's eyeballs nearly pop out of his head at this 'outlandish and unacceptable behaviour', and he uses this as concrete evidence that school is the 'best and only' place for us, especially Claude. And while he's saying all this with his back to her, the bump in the road pulls a face at him, and sticks out her tongue.

Later, at bedtime, Mum lies with us for a bit in our room, mainly because she knows Claude is furious and afraid. Her hair spreads out, dark against the white pillow and I think suddenly of our black shadows on the Zanzibar sand.

Claude's mouth is shut tight like a trapdoor. She is fuming.

'I'm sorry,' Mum says, and she squeezes our hands, and Claude breathes out long and slow like a hot-air balloon going down, down, down.

'What for?' I say, and Claude says, 'Yeah, which bit exactly?'

Mum doesn't say anything for a minute. Then she says, 'Coming back was the right thing to do.'

'So?' Claude says.

'And sometimes doing the right thing can be hard.'

Claude says something about how 'the right thing' is a matter of opinion actually, not a stone-cold truth. I am keeping out of it.

Mum says, 'But we did the kind thing. And that's always right, isn't it?'

'Kind to who?' Claude says, and then the three of us are very quiet for a bit, lying side by side on the bed and staring at the ceiling.

Claude's fury is still coming off her in waves, like the hot sun off tarmac.

I don't know what those two are thinking about while we lie there, but I'm thinking about brand new tiny turtles crawling out of their nests in the sand and following the moonlight into the sea, and swimming, swimming, swimming into the unknown, without stopping, and somehow knowing exactly where to go.

'I can't wait,' I whisper, and Mum squeezes my hand.

'I know,' Mum says.

'What if I can't do it?' Claude asks, and she covers her eyes with the back of her arm. My sister doesn't like people watching her cry.

Mum looks at me. I can see the whites of her eyes in the darkness. I have a good thought.

'Maybe this feels the same as before you go on a giant roller coaster or a high cliff dive,' I tell Claude.

She doesn't say anything, so I just carry on.

'You know how the first time you do it, you aren't sure how it will work out? But you do it anyway? And then after, you feel ten feet tall and like you can do *anything*.'

Mum squeezes my hand again, and Claude lets her arm slide down off her face. And I hope, more than any single thing I can think of in that moment, that I'm right.

When Mum says goodnight and leaves us alone in the street-light-orange dark, I say to my sister's silhouette, 'School won't beat us, Claude. It can't be that bad.'

She reaches out and strokes my arm, which is something she used to do in our other life, on camp-outs and car-journeys and night-boats, to help me fall asleep. I look over at her and I can see the shiny wet part of her eyes and the curved slope of her cheek, but not much more, and then she turns away from me to lie on her side and says, 'Well. I guess we are about to find out.'

9

That was two months ago, nearly. And now is now, and so much is different.

We have started school, and we are suddenly living like creatures of habit with rigid routines, like worker bees or daily commuters or Thomas Everyman Blake.

Claude gets up at the exact same time every day, Monday to Friday, and takes two buses to where she needs to be, in uniform, wearing a tie. Her new school timetable is split into hourly blocks and in between those blocks she says she is just trying to get from one place to another without being late. Being late is massively frowned upon in the universe called School. Being late, or untidy, or half asleep, are all wrong and Claude is turning out to be talented at all three of those things, almost to a professional level.

'Mind you,' she says. 'I am not the only one.'

The good news is that Claude is not finding school nearly as horrible or difficult as she thought she would. Her year is filled with people who are trying to stand out at the same time as trying to blend in. She says everyone wants to be different, but also the same, and she finds it kind of fascinating, in a watching-flies-lay-eggs-on-stuff kind of way.

She also says that it makes a change to spend time with people who are under 104.

She has started mentioning one or two people by name. Rizzle isn't as funny as he thinks he is, but lends her stuff when she forgets it. Leo is incredibly good at drawing. JoJo has been nice to her from Day One.

I am happy for Claude that she is already making friends.

So far, that makes one of us.

My school is just a short walk from Plane Tree Gardens, so I don't have to get up as early as Claude does, or catch any buses. I don't have to move about from lesson to lesson either, because everything happens in one room. But I am not enjoying myself. Not yet.

Here comes the next problem, looming on

the horizon like a tornado in Kansas. And guess who doesn't have glittery shoes she can click together so we can jet off and find a yellow brick road and a wizard behind a curtain? Guess who doesn't have any kind of get-out-of-jail-free card on her person at all?

School is not giving me that good 'After' feeling, as advertised. I am stuck at the 'Before'. Every day. Square One.

I want to do something about it, but there's a serious shortage of silver linings at the moment. School is a silver-lining-free zone. Grandad says, 'You'll get used to it,' like we are at the end of a conversation instead of the beginning.

Claude doesn't think I was built for school. She calls me *the wrong fit*. 'Like if you are the ugly sister, then school is the shoe,' she says, so

I sit there wondering if there is any chance at all it could be the other way round.

Mum says, 'It's bound to be a challenge,' and Dad ruffles my hair and says. 'You're still getting straight As in the school of life,' which makes Claude pretend to stick her fingers down her throat like she's going to puke, and is actually no help.

I was the one who was actually looking forward to school. I was genuinely, properly all geared up for it, and excited. But the truth is, school just feels all wrong to me, in more ways than I'd even thought possible. Quiet when it should be noisy, noisy when I'd prefer it to be quiet. There is a mind-boggling amount of crowd management, a lot of shouting about keeping our voices down. In assembly, the teachers use funny hand signals and everybody

a) automatically copies them and b) seems to know exactly what they mean, like a sign-language academy for robots. Everywhere smells like an airless cabin on a ship, two parts floor cleaner to one part wee.

It is stifling and overheated and I am constantly feeling like I can't get my breath.

Everything functions like one organism around me, apart from me. I have arrived at a colony, but I am the wrong kind of ant.

The head teacher thinks I am having difficulty adjusting.

This is not a thing that anyone has said about me before. Ever.

We have lived in hotels and mud huts and one marble villa and at least three types of van and travelled by plane and car and boat and train and sledge and camel and donkey. I have made friends in under twenty seconds with whole gangs of kids who don't speak the same language as me.

I am usually very good at change.

But the head teacher is right. And so is Claude.

I am having trouble. I do not fit. I am either the ugly sister, or the shoe. And there is no Fairy Godmother hovering in the corner of the playground, ready to turn a squashed juice box, a lost football and half a breakfast biscuit into some people who actually like me.

I have been the outsider before. But never like this.

People seem to be divided into clumps. I think I belong to the clump labelled 'new' and also maybe to 'weird', and definitely to 'haven't made our minds up about you yet'. I do not belong to the shiny clump called 'popular'. When I start trying to talk about the clumps with Claude, she says it's exactly the same at her school.

'It's social mobility in training,' she says, and I nod but, like most things that are happening to me at the moment, I don't think I know what that means.

She says, 'We don't stand a chance, not really, not straight away, because we are beginners and everyone else has been doing this since before they could read or even spell their own names.'

All I ask is for one person to be nice to me. I want to have one good day. But Claude shakes her head like I am reaching for the impossible. 'We are dealing with experts here, Joy. We can't expect to run before we can walk.'

Still, I can't help noticing that my sister doesn't seem to be having the same kind of problems as I am. She might have hated the idea of school before she got there, but since she started she is actually bordering on cheerful, for the first time in a while. Her brand new friends love the fact that that she can swear in nine different languages, but so far, that's not a skill that's working for anyone who sits near me.

My sister has taken to school like a duck to water, while I am still a fish out of it, flapping and flailing about on dry land. I am used to having good ideas about most things. But at the moment, I just don't know what I am supposed to do.

10

At my school, you have to ask before you can go to the loo. And believe it or not sometimes the answer is, 'No'. There are books for being tidy in and books for making mistakes, as if those two things didn't happen together, in the same place at the same time. For some unknown reason everyone steals the left-handed scissors, even when they are not left handed. Golden Time is the name for the last fifteen minutes of a Friday afternoon, which is the one and only chance you get to choose what you're doing and do your own thing. You have to earn Golden Time by doing exactly what you are told, all week. There are very strict times for work and for play, which are separate, and nobody else seems even the least bit bothered about the chances of being able to do both at once. Golden Time has not happened yet for me. Not once. This has a lot to do with my teacher, Mrs Hunter, and her evil dictatorship, otherwise known as class 6C.

I know for a fact that I am good at finding silver linings. I am brilliant at it. It is my special skill and my superpower. I have a nose for them, like the upside version of a bloodhound, or a truffle pig. I have been sniffing about for a while now in search of Mrs Hunter's. But for the first time in my life, I am very close to calling the search off, and officially announcing that I have nothing good to say. Not one thing.

I have never, in the history of ever, come to such a dead end before.

Mum says, 'She can't be all bad,' and I really am trying but I'm not so sure about that.

Mrs Hunter starts her day tired and cross and only gets crosser and more tired. She has one of those faces that looks furious even when she's thinking of something nice, because it's been furious so often. She does a lot of sighing. And she is officially, one hundred per cent in actual love with rules and regulations. They are her soulmate, the scaffolding to her building site, the stabilizer to her wheel. They complete her.

Sometimes, I wonder if she is human and

made of flesh and blood like other people, or just a different species altogether, built out of rules. Rules like no talking or running or singing or humming, unless you've been told specifically to talk or run or sing or hum. No getting up when you've had enough of being in one place and your body is losing its mind with the need to move. No laughing just because something is funny. No taking off your shoes when the book you are reading is so exciting and the classroom is so hot that your feet feel like they are about to explode. No interrupting or joining in or straying in any way from her idea of the script. No being happy. No expressing yourself. Red lights everywhere. Full stop.

I'm pretty sure that every single one of my new teacher's sentences starts with the word

NO, especially if the sentence in question is directed at me. Class 6C makes 48 Plane Tree Gardens look like a travelling circus, rowdy and chaotic, with Thomas Entertainer Blake in a crimson waistcoat and a top hat, twirling his walking stick, flanked by acrobats, leading the parade. Dad says there's a different silver lining in there somewhere, and I know there is, but that isn't making Monday to Friday daytimes any easier to take.

Mrs Hunter says that I am bad at listening and bad at keeping quiet and bad at reaching my full potential. She is all over the things I am bad at. I think she is focusing too much on those, and that she would like me a whole lot more if she thought about what I am actually good at. When I dare to make this suggestion, she looks like I have tried to feed her rotten fish while flicking hot chilli powder in her eye.

She pulls the same rotten-fish-with-chilli face when I tell her that reaching your full potential is technically impossible, because potential is always and only about what happens next. It is exactly the same as the end of the rainbow, which Claude has been reminding me since I was four years old that you can't actually reach. This fact about potential is what I would call interesting and Mrs Hunter would call cheeky. Cheeky is one of her top ten favourite words to use about me. I am trying not to remember the other nine.

It is hard being the school version of me. I don't know how I am supposed to spend another second sitting still and being quiet and keeping my shoes on at all times and not laughing at funny things. The thought of weeks and weeks of school fills me with absolute dread. These days I find myself wishing for moving day to come, even though I know full well that there is going to be no such thing.

11

The good thing about school is the playground, because it is out in the fresh air and there's a lot more room to breathe and move about. After the shoe-box classroom, it feels bigger than a football pitch, and the ceiling is infinite because it is made of the sky. You can stretch your arms over your head as far as they will possibly go without anybody even thinking about telling you

off. You can wake your
legs and feet up from their
long cross-legged sleep on
the carpet by walking round
and round the edges, right up against the high
brick wall. You can tip your head back and
look at the clouds and the criss-cross plane
trails and the dark underbellies of fat birds.

And the very best thing about it, my first
official piece of school silver lining, is right
there in the middle, impossible to miss. An
actual whopper, towering over everything else,
tearing up chunks of the heavy asphalt with its
roots, while its branches spread and its leaves
blink and roll and flutter in the wind.

If Claude was here she would roll her eyes
and give me a blank look and say, 'What, Joy?
It's just a tree.'

And it is.

An enormous oak tree with flat
stubby-fingered leaves that wave at
me from way up high while I am down
below feeling fish-out-of-water-ish and
alone. Somebody must have planted that
oak tree a very long time ago. Once, it
was a spindly sapling, bending in the

slightest wind, but now I can't get my arms all the way around its trunk. Now it is probably ancient, and the opposite of spindly, whatever the best word for that might be.

I lean my weight against its bark. Everybody in the playground is busy rushing around and screeching and throwing things, or huddled in clumps and whispering, or playing football or being a herd of ponies or sharing out chocolate buttons or laughing at something hilarious on a phone, but nobody is doing any of those things with me.

Only the tree is registering my existence. Only the tree is noticing me. That beautiful big oak is probably the friendliest living thing I have met since I started in class 6C, and I am very grateful.

Close to the trunk, the air is thick with green

shade and cool as fridges. The floor at my feet is littered with leaves and bits of twig like a forest, and the light flickers in and out with the fluttering leaves, and it is like another world under there, not a frantic school playground but somewhere else altogether, somewhere calm and soothing and un-lonely, where nobody but me has ever been.

For the first time in a while, I get a tingling in my fingers and all the hairs on my arms tickle and a big wide space opens up in my chest, because surely this is a real piece of magic, right here, big and solid and slap bang right in front of me. I realize too, in a sudden flash, that it is the exact thing I have been worrying about being, all this time – a seed, not allowed to go where the breeze takes it, but stuck in the ground, and forced to stay put and grow up in one single place.

And just look at it.

It is magnificent. Like a giant from a fairy tale, or an ancient king. It belongs in this playground. Its leaves are meant to dance far up above it while its roots muscle down way below. There is not a better place this tree could be.

I am marvelling at it, taking it all in, when something even more magical happens, something that floods me with relief like an incoming tide.

Somebody steps out of the hot tarmac sunshine and into the shady underneath of that big magic tree. It is a boy from 6C. I have seen him in the classroom a few times, out of the corner of my eye. He wears glasses and he is good at drawing and maths and Mrs Hunter doesn't seem to be all-day-long furious with him. I think his name is Benny.

He doesn't step into my silver lining by accident. He does it on purpose, definitely, and the reason I'm sure of this is that while he ducks under the lowest branches he is smiling straight at me.

'Hello,' he says. 'I'm Benny.'

'Joy,' I say, and I smile back and press my feet into the ground and put my hands in my pockets.

The light is shining directly on Benny's glasses so I can't see his actual eyes, I can only see a reflection of the tree, waving. I take this as a sign that he is the second friendliest living thing I have met today.

'What you doing?' he says, moving closer to stand by the trunk, and next to me.

'Nothing much,' I tell him. 'What about you?'

He grins at me. 'Nothing much.' Then he looks straight up into the branches, so that he is leaning right back. I can see the sides of his eyes now, and he has long dark eyelashes, and he is blinking.

'Isn't it amazing,' he says, still looking up, 'that this giant tree came from one teeny tiny acorn,' and he does this thing with his hand, like he is holding an acorn, no bigger than a thimble, between his finger and thumb. 'It's like everyday real-life magic.'

And that's when I am absolutely dazzled by silver linings, until I can hardly see.

12

Here is an example of what it is like to spend my time under the hawkish, all-seeing eye of Mrs Hunter.

Once upon a time, a girl called Joy gets into trouble for not finishing her description and diagram of a volcano for the big geography display.

Nobody lives happily ever after.

The end.

Mrs Hunter's side of that story is that I don't listen to instructions and I don't get on with my work and I absolutely fail to do as I am told. She says the rest of the class have managed to finish their writing and their volcano diagrams in time. Everyone else has their work displayed on the wall, but mine is missing because I didn't complete it. I don't deserve to be included, so as usual, and in a new and humiliating way, I am the one who gets left out.

My side of the story is quite different.

In mine, when Mrs Hunter tells us about the geography display, I say two things:

1. 'I love volcanoes,' and,
2. 'I've been inside one.'

By way of reply, my new teacher also says two things:

1. 'We don't talk without putting our hands up,' and,
2. 'In this class we tell the truth.'

'I am telling the truth,' I say, and then she blinks very slowly and purses her lips and does a thing with her hand across her mouth that is robot-school-sign-language for *zip it*.

In Iceland, I went right inside a dormant volcano with a very long name that I don't quite remember how to spell, but I know starts with Thrihnuk-. I have thought a lot about volcanoes and how they are so unbelievably hot that solid rock turns into a liquid and how that is going on in the centre of the Earth. All. Of. The. Time.

I have been to a place in Italy called Pompeii where, hundreds and hundreds of years ago, a volcano called Vesuvius erupted and turned everyone to stone. In Pompeii, you can see real people and dogs and horses running away and taking cover and maybe also just going about their day before they realized what was happening. All of them turned into statues. Instantly. By the sudden, hot, petrifying ash.

I'm not showing off when I say some of this to Mrs Hunter. I am just trying to have a conversation. I'm just into it. The planet's molten core is seething and bubbling like a hot sea or a witch's cauldron 24 hours a day way down beneath all of us while we lie in the park or get ready for work or stand in line at the supermarket or get told off for talking about it at school. That right there is what I mean by real magic. That is exactly the kind of thing that amazes me, that impresses me so easily, according to Claude.

It does not impress Mrs Hunter.

I actually know a lot of stuff about volcanoes, but Mrs Hunter only wants me to be quiet and copy some facts from a textbook, and not do any thinking of my own at all, just a boring diagram, same as everyone else's. She uses the cheeky word, again, and tells me to keep my hand down for at least half an hour.

I try to do what she tells me. I really do. But the quiet in 6C is not peaceful. It is the hold-your-breath kind of quiet that waits behind a door for something to go badly wrong, something terrible to happen. I can hear my own pulse and the scratch of pens and the clank of rulers, and the sixty-nostrilled dragon that is 6C breathing. Everybody is so unbearably good at staying still apart from me.

Benny looks up and tries to give me an encouraging look. He can't do it for long in case Mrs Hunter sees him. She very much frowns upon people doing any kind of talking or smiling or looking that she is not in charge of. He tries for half a second, and his eyes land on me and then glance off again, the way a butterfly does, light as a feather, always changing its mind. I try to say thank you without saying it, just by using my face. And then I keep my head down and try to be more like him, and do the best diagram possible, in the circumstances. But in my new enthusiasm, I manage to make a big scratch-hole in the paper, and half of my erupting volcano ends up on the actual desk, and to make matters worse I have been accidentally using the wrong marker pen, the one that doesn't wash off.

Mrs Hunter whinnies like a stung horse, while this time *everybody* watches. She says she will not tolerate graffiti and I will have to stay in for the whole of lunchtime to scrub it off. And even though my diagram still looks quite effective, with the hole in it and everything, it won't be going up on the display because she scrunches it up into a tight angry ball and makes me do the walk of shame across the classroom and put it in the bin.

A volcano is rumbling in my head. My arms and legs are all twitchy and restless, and the inside of my skull rolls and boils.

'What are we going to do with you, Joy?' Mrs Hunter says.

'I don't know,' I tell her, even though I do know exactly what we should do, which is get me out of that school and away from her as soon as possible.

The thought is hot as can be in the centre of my brain like the molten rock in the middle of the planet. I am standing on the sweaty carpet, clenching and unclenching my fists, grinding my teeth the way Claude does, and trying to breathe.

'Back to your seat,' she barks, looking down at something on her lap and not at me.

I keep my fists clenched and my jaw tight shut and I put one foot in front of the other, not in the direction of my chair, but the other way, towards the door.

From behind me, her voice says, 'And where do you think you are going?'

Sometimes, when I'm supposed to be listening, or doing pages full of sums, or spelling tests, I think about what my days would be like if I could just be out in the world and learning things the way I like to learn them, the way I always have, which doesn't involve sitting still like a statue until I think my eyeballs are going to burst, or listening to Mrs Hunter's endless instructions, or getting told which rule I have already broken three hundred times before lunch and being made to feel about as small and as welcome as a gnat.

'*Out,*' I tell her.

The sixty-nostrilled dragon gasps, and Benny looks up at me and his mouth is a big round O and then he SMILES, just when I feel like the opposite of smiling, and before I can even try to smile back even a little, the door bangs shut behind me and the glass in it that rattles is criss-crossed with threads of metal, like a cage.

Outside in the corridor, the floors are polished to a high shine and even though I can hear a kind of buzzing from inside 6C, like a nest of wasps, it is eerily silent. An abandoned school in a ghost town. My own breathing is super-loud in my ears while I walk and other voices drift from behind other classroom doors, but the voices aren't talking to me. Any minute now, I think Mrs Hunter is going to come bursting out of 6C after me, like the monsters I imagine behind me in the dark. My lava feet carry me to the fire-door behind reception that leads out onto the playground.

Right now it's a good thing there's no magic at all in my family, because if there was, even a shred, I would use it to make Mrs Hunter and all of her hundreds and thousands of rules grow tails and snouts and ears and go snorting off into the distance, far, far away.

By myself in the playground, I go straight to the base of the oak tree and take a big green shady breath. I close my eyes for the count of three, and then I start to climb. I don't stop until I reach the cradle at the centre of its branches, more than halfway up, where I sit in a shallow bowl big enough to fit me, like I'm sitting in the palm of its giant hand. It feels safe and sturdy and gentle, this great big, solid, unmoveable thing. The light through the leaves is dappled and dancing, and I am up high enough to feel like I belong to its arms and the sky, and not the ground, not the classroom, definitely not Mrs Hunter any more. The bark under my hands is puckered and wrinkled like an elephant's hide, and not far from where I am sitting, someone has carved a heart into it about the size of my thumb. Soft and damp in places with the mulch of old leaves, home to about a million different bugs, it smells of rich dark earth and mildewed books and the sweetest freshest air, all at the same time.

I hear the fire-door clank and slam and when I look down I can see the top of Mrs Hunter's head, slightly backcombed, stuck with pins. She marches across the playground underneath me, looking angrier than ever, and her shoes make a snapping sound on the tarmac. The sight of her makes me unhappy. I think *she* is unhappy and her unhappiness is catching.

So for a minute, I stop looking down.

I look up.

At the underside of a pigeon, bluey-smooth and slate grey, hook-beaked and busy-eyed.

At the veins on the leaves, plump with water, spread like roadmaps.

At the fine, reaching tips of the furthest branches.

Way below me, the footsteps stop.

'Joy Applebloom,' Mrs Hunter says. 'Where are you?'

I shift a little bit in my tree, and I think about not answering, but then I know that will just get me in more trouble. So I say, 'Up here,' and she turns her face up to me, and her mouth opens and shuts like a carp's, and for the first time that I can think of, she is actually lost for words. Her frown disappears, smooths right out until she looks almost kind, probably out of shock at my terrible behaviour, and before she can remember how to tell me to, I start climbing back down.

13

For the rest of the day, I do my schoolwork in the head teacher's office. This is supposed to be a punishment but it doesn't feel like one at all. It is a nice kind of quiet in there. The carpet doesn't smell of anything horrid and there are lots of pot-plants and even more paintings. For most of the afternoon, once she has finished shout-whispering at me, it is a Mrs-Hunter-free zone. And whenever I feel like it, I can just look up and out of the window, and straight at my new favourite tree.

The head teacher's name is Miss Stilwell. She has large brown eyes and very sleek blond hair that looks like she has ironed it, or kept it overnight between the pages of a heavy book. When she talks to me, she knits her fingers together, over and under, in and out. Four of them have thin gold rings on. I like Miss Stilwell. She asks lots of questions and she is better at listening than Mrs Hunter will ever be. She says things like, 'What else is different?' and 'How can we help?' and she asks me about Claude and Mum and Dad and Grandad, and she actually pays attention to my answers. Miss Stilwell is the third unexpected silver lining I have found so far at school.

When she picks up the phone and calls 48 Plane Tree Gardens, she doesn't say I've been bad or disobedient or untrustworthy, or a loose cannon. She doesn't use any of the words about me that Mrs Hunter would. She just says, 'Joy has had a difficult day. Perhaps you could come and have a chat with me about it at pick-up time.' And when she puts the phone back down she smiles, and asks her secretary to get me a drink and a biscuit.

'You're very good at climbing trees,' she says, and I say, 'Thank you. I've practised a lot.'

Then she asks me if I have visited a lot of forests, and she leans forward a little bit, like she actually wants to hear my answer. So I tell her about the Amazon Rainforest and the Crooked Forest in Poland. I tell her we have walked in the Canadian Great Bear Forest and camped in the Cloud Forest in Costa Rica. I explain that cloud forests get their name from the weather, because it is always cloudy and all sorts of species of plant and animal and insect like to live there.

She asks me if I have a favourite tree, but it is very hard to decide between a Californian Redwood that is so big it looks like it belongs on a different planet, or a Jacaranda which has really lovely bright purple flowers, or a Banyan, whose roots grow down through the air until they hit the ground and turn into new trunks, or the Gingko which has leaves as big as umbrellas and might actually be the oldest tree ever in the history of the world.

'Perhaps you could do a project of your own,' Miss Stilwell says. 'About your travels.

Some of your favourite places, some of the best places you have been.'

'I'd like that,' I tell her, and then she says, 'So would I.'

When Dad comes to get me, he goes into Miss Stilwell's office to have a chat with her, and she asks if I would like to take a seat outside. The school secretary, Mr Gibson, raises his eyebrows at me. I sit right by the door and lean a bit back in my own chair to get my ear closer, though I can't hear what they actually say.

I am sitting there, having to mind my own business, when Benny walks past the doorway, whistling. Benny is a good whistler. His whistle is loud and clear and sharp. He walks past and then the whistling stops and Benny backs up so that he is in the doorway again. He waves at me, and I wave back, sort of down low, because I don't know if I'm allowed and I don't want Mr Gibson to raise his eyebrows at me again.

In the hand that isn't waving, Benny is holding a piece of paper that has been scrunched up and then flattened back out. I can see the wrinkle lines all over it. It is my volcano drawing, and he has rescued it from the bin. He takes two steps into the office and gives it back to me, and then he takes two steps back again.

'Oh, thanks,' I say. 'Thank you so much.'

'You're welcome,' Benny says. 'It's really good.'

And then, right there in the doorway, he does an impression of Mrs Hunter that is so funny it actually hurts. He sticks out his bum

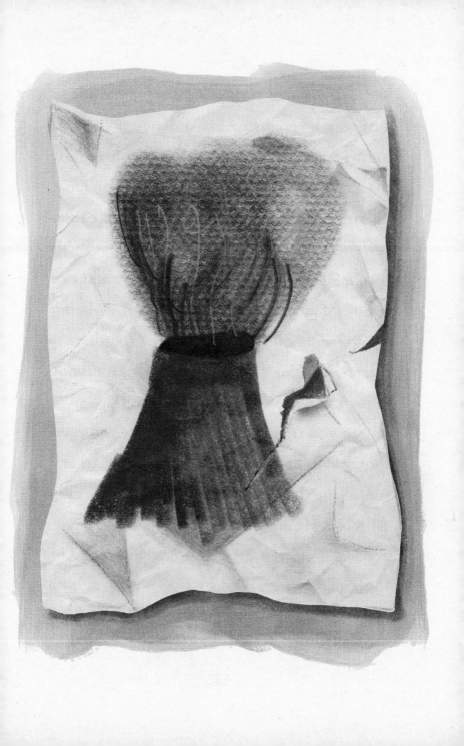

and narrows his eyes and pulls his mouth in a tight, puckered ring like a done-up PE bag, until I am curled up like a bug in my chair from too much laughing, and Mr Gibson must be starting to wonder if I have choked on my ginger nut. I am Joy, almost dying of joy, and because I am trying to hold it in, and not annoy Miss Stilwell and Dad who are being very serious on the other side of the door, I can feel my laugh zipping and rocketing about in my insides like popping candy.

'See you tomorrow,' Benny says. And even though I am sitting outside the head teacher's office and I am in bigger trouble than ever with Mrs Hunter, and Mr Gibson's beady eyes are watching me, I just cannot wipe the big beaming smile off my face.

* * *

On the way home, Dad is quiet, but he gets me an ice cream, so I figure he's not all that cross. I tell him my side of the volcano diagram story, and he says, 'It's okay, Joy. I know it's tough. I'm sure you're doing your best. I think we all are.'

Mum is at the front door when we get back and she gives me a hug. She says, 'I'm sorry you had a bad day at school.'

'I didn't,' I say.

'Oh?'

'I had a good day.'

'Really? You did?'

She and Dad look at each other over my head. I can always tell when they are doing that because they go very quiet at the same time and forget to keep breathing.

'It was actually the best day so far,' I tell them.

'Joy,' Dad says. 'You walked out of class in the middle of a lesson.'

'Yes. Mrs Hunter made me throw my work in the bin.'

'Did she?'

'Yes.'

'How awful.'

'You got sent to the head teacher.'

'Yep.'

'For the whole afternoon.'

'It doesn't sound like a very good day to me,' Mum says, and Dad says, 'Me neither.'

I take an apple from the fruit bowl. 'I made a friend,' I say.

'Did you?' they say together.

'Yep. His name is Benny and we met under my new favourite tree and he is very funny and really kind and extremely good at impressions.

He has curly black hair and he wears glasses and he is really excellent at maths and he gave me my diagram back. Look, here it is.'

I hand them the wrinkly bit of paper with the hole in it. They lean their heads together while they look at it.

Mum says, 'It's very good,' and Dad says, 'That volcano really looks like it erupted.'

'I know,' I said. 'Benny got it out of the bin for me. And now I am really looking forward to going to school tomorrow.'

'Good for you, Joy,' Dad says, and Mum tells me I am right, and that it has been a pretty good day after all.

'I haven't even told you everything about the tree yet,' I say, and they say they'd like to hear all about it at supper, which is going to be pea and pesto pasta with parmesan which is my absolute favourite kind of pasta there is.

For the first half of supper time everyone else is mostly talking about Claude's table manners, so I don't get a chance to tell anyone about the tree. After she has patted me on the back for making my first friend, Claude is not interested in any of the chosen topics of conversation. She rolls her eyes at the grown-ups and keeps her mouth mostly shut unless food is going in it. She's got one earphone in. The other one dangles over her plate on its string like a stretched-out bit of gum. I don't know what she is listening to, but I do know she isn't planning to stop. Mum and Dad and most definitely Grandad don't want her to have any earphones in and she wants to have two. Only one earphone is Claude meeting them halfway.

When Thomas Ear-Trumpet Blake tries to read her the riot act about devices at the table, Mum puts her hand on his and says, 'Not now, Dad,' and he grips his knife and fork like his life depends on it, and says, 'Well, then when?'

To change the subject, I try to start a conversation with Grandad about oak trees and he's actually really interested. He leans forward in his chair and the corners of his mouth twitch, like they are getting ready to smile.

'Do you know a lot about oak trees?' I ask him.

'*Quercus robur*,' Thomas Encyclopaedia Blake says. 'The British oak?'

'Yes,' I say. 'I think so. I met one today.'

'*Met* one?'

'Yes. In the school playground.'

And I tell him about the giant oak with its trunk way wider than my arms can even reach and its flat-fingered leaves and its branches as thick as elephants' trunks. I tell him about sitting high up in it above the playground and thinking about what else there used to be all around it when it was no bigger than me.

'Are you allowed to climb trees in the playground?' he says, and I tell him, 'No. But that's a different story.'

I am remembering what Benny said about a teeny-tiny acorn and how amazing it is, when Grandad says, 'That is actually quite a famous tree. And you're right. It's very, *very* old. Even older than me.'

'Not possible,' Claude says, because she can still hear us, even though she's trying not to.

Grandad gives her the quickest of looks and

then turns his attention back to my tree. 'Some people think it is in the Domesday Book.'

'*Really?*' Mum says, and I say, 'What's that?'

Claude puts her second earphone in and turns up the sound. Dad starts clearing the table. Mum gets up to help him, and while she's doing it, she says, 'The Domesday Book is a sort of survey of everything in the country'.

Grandad leans even more forward in his chair. 'Done by William the Conqueror,' he says. 'In 1086.'

'*1086?*' I say. 'That's like a thousand years ago.'

He nods. 'Some people think that your tree is mentioned in it, and some disagree. It's a hot topic at the local Historical Society.'

Claude must still be able to hear us because she bends forward so that her face is on the table. She is pretend snoring.

'At the what?' I ask.

'We meet sometimes and talk about the past,' Grandad tells me. 'I'm sure I have a pamphlet about it somewhere. Now where have I put that?'

He goes to look for it and my sister groans and staggers out of the room as if we are literally poisoning her with boredom. But I'm not bored. I am the opposite. My heart is beating and my pulse is ticking and my smile is invading my whole face like it's William the Conqueror and I am 1086.

Because as if making friends with Benny isn't enough of a silver lining to be happy about, I might have also just made friends with an actual thousand-year-old tree.

14

The next day is Friday and I am beyond excited to see Benny again because I have so much to tell him. I am awake at almost the same time as Thomas Excellent Blake, who seems surprised in a good way to see me up, and makes me a cup of tea with two sugars without being asked. Even Buster is nicer than normal and wraps himself around my ankles once or twice before he goes out.

I am ready for school more than a whole hour before I need to be, so I read Grandad's Historical Society pamphlet again, and I look up *oak* in the big downstairs-loo tree encyclopaedia - genus *quercus robur*, so I can brush up on my facts.

There is an oak tree in Nottingham Forest that used to know Robin Hood. There is one in Lincolnshire whose trunk is so wide that it has been hollowed out and filled with chairs to make a dining room. There are two two-thousand-year-old oaks named after giants in Glastonbury that used to mark the entrance into Avalon. And there is my tree, the Domesday Book tree in the playground, my first school silver lining, the place I met Benny, and hid from Mrs Hunter, and looked out over the rooftops while I sat in the palm of its thousand-year-old hand.

Benny sits next to me on the carpet and even though we have to stare straight ahead and pay attention to what Mrs Hunter is talking about, I can tell by the way his elbow bumps against mine every now and then that he has been looking forward to seeing me too. Benny pushes his glasses into place every four minutes, and every four minutes they slide back down his nose. He bites his lip when he is thinking and he has a frown between his eyebrows that looks exactly like a comma. He is very good at sitting still and very good at concentrating and when he puts his hand up, Mrs Hunter almost looks like she is smiling, and picks him to give the answer, which is the opposite of what happens when that happens to me.

But today I am really good in class and I sit mind-bendingly, jaw-achingly still and I don't put my hand up once and I don't make a peep and instead I finish a really long piece of comprehension about a girl called Sally buying sultana muffins from the wrong shop.

Mrs Hunter spends the morning looking like she has lost something, and I suspect that the thing she has lost is any kind of reason to be cross with me.

At break, even though five boys ask him to play football, and three girls offer him some of their strawberry laces, Benny and I go straight to the quiet shady underneath of our tree. Together. My smile is all stretchy and stuck on my face.

Benny says, 'Have you really been to all those places?' and I tell him a little bit about where we have lived and how we have always blown about like seeds, and how now we have landed at Plane Tree Gardens because of Grandad. I tell him about Claude and Mum and Dad. I say that this is the first time I have been to a real school in my life and that's why I'm not doing so well at it.

Benny says, 'Wow.' A lot. And he also says, 'Oh, you're doing fine.'

Then it is my turn to ask questions, and this is some of what I manage to learn about Benny at first break.

His full name is Benjamin Eddison Hooper. He lives with his brother and his mum and dad in the big flats that I can see from my bedroom window. There are three blocks and they have different names and different colour rooftops and Benny's block is called Sunningdale and it is yellow.

'Yellow is my favourite colour,' he says. 'So it was meant to be.'

Benny has lived at number 114 in Sunningdale his whole life. His mum is an artist and she makes jewellery and she works in the canteen at school. I know exactly who she is without him having to tell me, because she has a big smile and she gave me extra big portions on my first day and when I think about it she looks a bit like Benny if he didn't wear glasses and had braids in his hair.

Benny says I am very lucky to have lived in so many different places. He loves to travel too. His favourite place in the world so far is his grandparents' house on a hillside in the Blue Mountains in Jamaica. He and his Mum and his brother go there every summer and he thinks it is paradise.

Benny Hooper is the fastest runner in the school and the Under-Eleven's County Chess Champion. He plays the violin. He might want to be an archaeologist when he is older because he likes digging stuff up. He thinks there is hidden treasure everywhere if you know where to look for it. 'A bit like silver linings on clouds,' is how he puts it, and I can't stop smiling again.

He says, 'My brother thinks that I call everything treasure and that muddy old coins aren't anything to get worked up about.'

He says, 'My brother thinks I am way too easily impressed.'

I say, 'Your brother should meet my sister. I think they'd be friends.'

After break, Mrs Hunter puts us into pairs to do a local history project, and to my surprise, she puts me in a pair with Benny. I have no idea if this is the first nice thing Mrs Hunter has ever done for me or if it is a total accident, but it doesn't matter because either way, I am delighted.

There are local newspapers and print-outs from the internet and some pamphlets like Grandad's and some books with photos of what the streets and houses looked like when there weren't so many cars and people wore glasses shaped like angels' wings and buttoned their coats all the way up. I wonder if Mrs Hunter is a member of the same local Historical Society as Grandad, but I don't ask her because I'm afraid she will think I'm being cheeky and I'm also a bit afraid that her answer will be, 'Yes.'

Benny and I know what our project will be about without even having to think about it.

We are going to draw the trunk and branches of our oak tree and then stick on lots of interesting facts about it in the shapes of acorns and flat-fingered leaves. It is going to be a local history collage, going back a thousand years. I want to start with the drawing, but Benny says we should get the historical facts bit out of the way first, because that way we can do the work and then finish with the fun part. I am starting to think that he might be the cleverest person I know. We need eight facts because we realize that we both have a favourite number – eight! Also it will look nice and symmetrical on the page.

'There is the Domesday Book fact,' I say, 'for a start,' and Benny says, 'And the how long the school has been here fact, which is 167 years.'

'There's the year-in-the-life-of-the-oak-tree

fact,' he says, which we both know isn't local history at all, and more like science, but is so interesting we have decided to use it anyway.

6C is a hive of activity, and for once I feel like I am part of it.

Mrs Hunter walks past us. I keep my head down but she stops and drops a folded newspaper down on the desk.

'This has some news about your tree in it,' she says, and Benny picks it up and says, 'Thank you,' and I keep it zipped, because I know she prefers me that way.

'What nice manners, Benny,' she says, and she looks down her nose at me before she moves to the next desk, where Bailey and Jawad are talking about doing their project on the history of school meals.

Benny is rifling through the paper looking

for the oak tree and when he finds it he smiles and then after that all the colour drains straight out of his face and he just says, 'OH.'

'What is it?' I say.

Benny opens the paper and flattens it out so I can see it too.

'The council is going to build a fancy new school,' he says.

'Oh, that's good,' I say, but his face isn't agreeing with me. 'Isn't it?'

'No, it isn't,' he says. 'It's terrible.'

'Why?'

For a minute, I think this is another thing about school that I just don't understand.

Benny points at the paper. He hits it with the back of his hand while he is talking, so it goes *thwack-thwack-thwack* like Mrs Hunter's shoes.

'They are going to need to chop our tree down,' he says. 'That's why.'

My head is pounding. The volcano is back. I think of the soft bowl, like the palm of its hand, and the green light, and all the life in it, all the hundreds and hundreds of years.

'*What*?' I say, and then I say it again, but louder.

Benny puts the paper under both our noses and suddenly I am face to face with a picture of Miss Stilwell standing by the oak tree, shaking hands with the mayor and holding up a picture of a futuristic new building that could surely go somewhere else without hurting anything, and is not going to destroy one measly acorn if I have anything to do with it.

'That can't happen,' I tell him.

152

Benny's hunches his shoulders and pushes out his bottom lip. 'But it most likely will though.'

'No,' I say. 'We can't let it,' and when I look up, I am shocked to see Mrs Hunter watching me with a sad, sorry smile.

Benny has his back to her. He watches me too, over the top of his slipped-down glasses. The frown-comma between his eyebrows is as deep as if someone carved it with a penknife into the trunk of a tree.

'It's the school and the council and the builders and everything,' he says, 'and we are just *us*. What can *we* do?'

'There must be *rules*,' I say. 'Surely? To protect famous old trees?'

Benny is looking very downtrodden and defeated. 'I don't know.'

'Well, let's find out,' I say. 'We can look it up. And I can ask my grandad.'

'Really?'

'He knows about a lot of things,' I say. 'He's quite old and historical. It's worth a try.'

Benny shrugs.

We carry on cutting out pieces of paper in the shape of oak leaves, and while I am cutting I am quiet and I am thinking.

I have made friends with all sorts of trees in all sorts of places. I have probably climbed at least seventeen different kinds. I have stayed high up in a treehouse and fallen asleep to the *scritch-scratch* of other creatures and the *shushing* of the leaves.

Benny is right. We are just us. And that isn't all that much.

But *everybody* knows how important trees

are. They clean the air and give us oxygen. They protect us from the sun. They feed us and other animals. They provide warmth and shelter and shade. We actually seriously couldn't live without trees.

Maybe some people have forgotten that. Maybe we should remind them.

We make eight leaves and six acorns, so that we have some spare ones if we make a mistake. And then I put the left-handed scissors down and say to Benny, 'We have to do something.'

'Yes.'

'We're small, but we're not nobody,' I say.

'True.'

'And something is always better than nothing,' I tell him.

Benny pushes his glasses up his nose and

blinks at me. He is already looking a bit more cheerful and optimistic.

'You're right,' he says. 'Let's make a plan.'

15

On Saturday afternoon I meet Benny at the library and we use the photocopier. We have to get special tokens from the librarian at the counter, and he says, 'What are you two up to?' in a smiley, the opposite of Mrs Hunter way, and I tell him we are going to save a tree.

'Well, that's very noble,' he says.

'So is the tree,' we tell him, and on the way

out, Benny gives him one of our photocopies and he reads it and gives us the thumbs up and says, 'Best of luck.'

On Sunday night, I have to wait for everyone to go to sleep, even Claude. I want to tell her about the plan, but Benny thinks we should be extra-secretive and extra-careful until it happens, so I keep it all in. I listen to her breathing, and the bathroom taps going on and off, and the loo flushing. I count three different sets of footsteps walking about. And then after it goes quiet, I wait for a bit before I get out of bed and creep downstairs. Mum and Dad are asleep on the sofa bed and Dad is snoring like a wart hog and neither of them hears me opening the back door and bringing back some old bits of cardboard from the shed. I lay everything out on the kitchen floor, and I start painting. I am as alert as a meerkat, and quieter than a mouse, and I know for a fact that a few streets away, at 114 Sunningdale, Benny is busy doing the exact same thing.

I make two big signs and I write the words loud and bold. Each letter is the size of my hand.

I make one rubbish sandwich, because it is surprisingly hard to cut bread and open and shut cupboards and clear up crumbs at the same time as being totally silent. Stuffing ginger nuts into a paper bag in a sleeping house feels loud enough to wake the whole street, and when I fill Grandad's ancient tartan flask with water, I whisper to the tap to please stop gurgling and just get on with it.

Buster is very interested in what I am up to. He

purrs like a finely tuned engine while I tell him what I think about anyone chopping down any tree, anywhere, never mind a possibly thousand-year-old one in my school playground.

The plane trees might be long gone from around here, but if I have anything to do with it, that ancient oak is here to stay.

One thousand years, I remind myself. And then I hide the painted signs and the food and water by the bins inside the front gate, and go back to bed. I am not exactly sure when I spill the red paint on Grandad's hall carpet. It looks a bit like blood. When I notice, I put one of Dad's shoes on top of it and carry on with what I'm doing. I know I will be worrying about red paint stains later, but I just don't have time for that now.

I wait patiently all night for the sun to come

up. And when it finally does, the morning routine at Plane Tree Gardens is exactly the same as usual. In the kitchen with Grandad, I yawn and stretch and pretend that I have only just woken up, and I think I am quite convincing. Claude notices Dad's shoe all alone in the middle of the hallway, and I whisper at her to please not move it and that I don't have time to tell her when or why.

'What's underneath?' she says.

'Red paint.'

'Oh, wow, Joy,' she says. 'I wouldn't want to be you today.'

'You never want to be me,' I tell her, and she shrugs and says, 'Yeah. True.'

Mum says something about me being ready for school earlier and earlier, and I tell her that I am doing my best not to annoy Mrs Hunter any more. I cross my fingers behind my back while I am saying this, because it is not actually true, not to mention impossible.

'And how's your new friend?' she says, winking, and I say, 'He's fine,' and Claude says, 'Mum. Is there something wrong with your eye?'

'I think Joy is turning over a new leaf,' Dad says, and I smile.

'Something like that.'

Claude and I leave at the same time. Dad waves goodbye and when he shuts the door, I duck back quickly and pick up the stuff by the bins.

'What's all that?' Claude says. 'What are you up to?' Then her face goes all still and she says, 'You're not running away are you?'

'Of course not!' I say.

She blows the air out of her mouth, like *phew*, and says, 'Good. For a minute there...'

'I would never do that,' I tell her. 'Not without telling you.'

'So what are you doing, then?'

Between Grandad's gate and her bus stop, I explain to Claude about the tree and how Benny and I are going to try and save it.

'Good for you,' she says, and then she kisses me on the cheek for the first time in ages, which is nice, and says, 'Don't get expelled,' which isn't.

The signs are tricky to carry because they are hard to keep a grip on and quite heavy and the edges keep digging into my side. I have to stop and start a lot but I still get to school about half an hour early, which is just about perfect. Mr

Gibson hasn't opened the gates yet so I duck out of sight behind a white van, and I keep the signs turned the wrong way and close to my chest. The white van has something about trees written on the back and there are two men in the front with the windows down and they look like they are waiting for the school gates to open too. I have a look through the back windows and there are tools and neon overalls and massive chainsaws in there.

Benny appears behind the van too, out of nowhere. One of his signs says NO!!! and the other one says WAY!!! in glossy black letters as big as my head.

'*Look*,' I say, pointing madly at the back of the van, and Benny peers in and then says, 'Ouch.'

'Do you think it's *today*?' I ask him. 'Do you

think they are here to chop it down? *Already?'*

He grips his signs even tighter. 'I don't know,' he says, all serious and determined. 'But if it was supposed to happen today, it isn't going to any more.'

The gates open, and the men get out of the van and go through the playground with Mr Gibson towards the school office. Benny and I wait for the first one or two families to trickle in and then we make a run for it to the other side of the oak's trunk. With our bags on our backs, passing the signs up to each other, we climb, higher than I was before, until we are looking out over the scrap of grey playground and the puddle-wet, lost-property rooftops of school. I count three hula-hoops, four tennis balls, two frisbees and a shoe, and I'm not even trying. The brooding block of the temporary classroom looks like an enormous out-of-order caravan, probably because it more or less is. And the old markings on the playground for hopscotch and tennis and netball and football are hardly there now, just very faint, like jellyfish in the water, or those wispy high kinds of clouds, or tired ghosts.

Nobody sees us. I am starting to wonder if this oak tree is invisible. But there is no storybook magic involved, not really, apart from the astonishing trick of everybody being fantastically unobservant and not seeing what's right in front of their very own eyes, which is a girl and a boy, that happen to be me and Benny, squatting in the top branches like over-sized pigeons, waving signs around that say, NO!!! and, WAY!!! and, OLD AND MAGIC!!! and, PLEASE SAVE THIS TREE!!!!

The playground fills and empties like a rock pool as wave after wave of parents bring their barnacle kids through the gates. The early ones take their time, the late ones shout goodbyes over their shoulders without looking, and try not to drop everything while they run in. We watch them go past and right underneath us, watch their unseeing faces and the very tops of their heads. When the bell rings, the rock pool organizes itself into lines for each classroom, and all the teachers come out of the building to stand at the front.

'Ready?' Benny says, and I nod, and we start waving our signs around and yelling at the top of our voices.

'SAVE OUR TREE! SAVE OUR TREE!'

The teachers' heads snap up like turtles and the lines of children turn, and then someone is pointing, and mouths are dropping open, and people who aren't teachers are saying things behind their hands and everyone seems to be starting to realize what's going on high above them in the branches. The line that is 6C has got all bedraggled and Mrs Hunter is caught between whipping it back into shape and trying to see what's happening. She wants to know what all the fuss is about, and any minute now she is going to see that all the fuss

is about Benny and me.

'NOW!' Benny shouts, and we drop our photocopies at the same time, loads of them, all cut out in the shape of oak leaves, and they float and drift to the floor way below us like it is suddenly autumn and it is really quite clever and beautiful.

PLEASE SAVE THIS TREE!

PLEASE SAVE THIS TREE!

PLEASE SAVE THIS TREE!

PLEASE SAVE THIS TREE!

PLEASE SAVE THIS E!

PLEASE SAVE THIS TREE!

PLEASE
SAVE THIS
TREE

Benny high-fives me and we shout some more 'SAVE OUR TREE's. And then the lines in the playground break wide open and everyone is running and ducking to pick up our leaflets and the teachers are huffing and puffing like steam trains. Some of the grown-ups from drop-off are still here, with their phones out, taking pictures. Benny and I waggle our signs and all around us the leaves waggle like they are holding signs too. Mrs Hunter is staring straight at us with her piercing gaze and I feel it in the pit of my stomach, like a boulder, all the trouble I am going to be in. She reaches into her handbag and takes out a phone and I wonder if she is actually going to get us in the biggest trouble of all and call the police. I'm sure the oak tree isn't nearly as worried about Mrs Hunter as I am. I bet she is just a dot on the landscape. It has most likely seen bigger battles than this, with horses and bows and arrows and suits of armour and buckets and buckets of blood. The only blood in sight now is from a small cut on my thumb that happened when I was climbing up and trying to carry everything without making too much fuss. We are still chanting. I grip my sign until my knuckles go tight and my jaw feels like a steel trap and I try to look as strong and powerful as possible.

And then the strangest thing happens. It is over so quickly that I'm not sure if it's real.

But I swear I see Mrs Hunter quickly raise a fist and shake it, like she's with us, like she's actually on our side.

'Did you see that?' Benny says, and I say, 'Mrs Hunter doing a fist-pump?' and he says,

'Yes,' and we both say, 'Wow.'

Miss Stilwell comes out of the school building with Mr Gibson in tow. Her hair is still sleek and pale but her face is more like the colour of a beetroot, and the words are bursting like lid-off popcorn from her mouth. They march to the very bottom of the tree, moving the gaggle of up-lookers out of their path like a snow plough.

'COME DOWN AT ONCE!' Miss Stilwell shouts up at us.

Behind them, over by the fire door, the men in their fluorescent jackets are lurking with their hands in their pockets.

'NO WAY!' we shout back down.

'It is VERY UNSAFE,' she shouts, and I tell her, 'I am a VERY GOOD tree climber.'

'What if you FALL?' she says, and Benny

says, 'We are very comfortable here and we are NOT MOVING.'

'This is NOT THE WAY to do this,' Miss Stilwell says, speaking through her cupped hands.

'WHO ARE THOSE MEN?' shouts Benny, and Mr Gibson says something to her behind his hand, and she shouts, 'They're from the COUNCIL.'

'If we come DOWN,' Benny yells, 'so will the TREE. We're not STUPID. We weren't born YESTERDAY.'

Miss Stilwell pops and sputters. She calls Mrs Hunter over and they talk about something that we can't hear from up here, and Miss Stilwell looks extremely cross. I never expected to see Mrs Hunter get told off, ever. She is trying to look sorry and serious, but I swear she's got a bit of a glint in her eye. Something silver.

All the children get taken inside by the teachers until the only people left in or above the playground are me and Benny and Miss Stilwell and Mr Gibson and the men from the council.

Then Mr Gibson is shouting at us again but Benny and I can't hear him because we are still chanting at the top of our voices, and if we weren't holding onto big signs we would have our hands over our ears to make a point.

The men in charge of chainsaws look at each other and go and sit in their van.

Benny and I stay in the tree for so long that our arms and legs start to go all stiff, like its branches.

I say. 'I think I might actually be turning into a tree.'

There are loads of faces at the classroom windows, all squashed up and crowded in, and all the kids are waving and calling things and grinning at us and pulling funny faces through the glass.

'They aren't allowed out at break because of us,' says Benny.

'Do you think they mind?'

He shrugs. 'Not really.'

I tell him I'm not going to lose any friends because I haven't really made any.

Benny smiles and his teeth are very neat and very straight. 'Oh, everyone is going to want to be your friend now you're famous.'

His glasses shine the sun straight back at me, and he looks like he is practically made of silver linings, and I could not be more delighted.

'Do you think so?'

'For a fact,' he says, and then he waggles the sign again, because there is someone else down below us, someone who has just come into the playground, with polished shoes and a brown jacket and thin grey hair that looks like plastic with a dusting of cement.

I could not be more surprised about it if I tried.

He introduces himself loudly to Miss Stilwell, using his full name, which is Thomas Ernest Blake. Mystery solved.

Just as loudly, he says, 'I am a founder member of the local Historical Society, and I am here to offer my support and expertise to this campaign.'

'What campaign?' Miss Stilwell says.

'The campaign to save this ancient and valuable tree.'

Benny claps his hands together. '*Yes,*' he says, repeating the words. 'Ancient and Valuable.'

Miss Stilwell is asking Grandad how he even knows about this 'so-called *campaign*'.

'The Historical Society was contacted anonymously,' he says, sounding very busy and important, 'by telephone. And anyway, I think you will find this is already all over social media.'

My mouth is wide open like I'm catching flies. I didn't know my grandad even knew what social media was.

'Who *is* that?' Benny says.

'Thomas Ernest Blake,' I tell him.

'Do you know him?'

'Well, yes,' I say. 'I met him recently.'

'Where?'

'He's my grandad.'

Benny laughs and we shout 'SAVE OUR TREE!' again, and down below, Thomas Ernest Blake picks up one of our oak leaflets and reads what is written on it, which is this:

This tree is more than a thousand years old. Some people think it was recorded in the Domesday Book in 1086. It gives food and shelter to loads of different bugs and animals and people. At night it sucks in carbon dioxide and it breathes out oxygen. It has worked very hard from its beginnings as an acorn. It is the best thing about our school. Please build a new one around it instead of on top of it.

Then he looks up at us through all the branches and leaves and he waves our leaflet about and shouts, 'Very interesting. Very well done, you two. Very good indeed,' and he picks up six or seven more.

'Perhaps we should step inside your office and telephone the council,' he says to Miss Stilwell in the politest of voices.

She points up at us nervously. 'This is a health and safety issue,' she says, and then Grandad says, 'Well, may I suggest that somebody gets a tall ladder?'

Mr Gibson runs off to find the caretaker, and Grandad gives a leaflet to Miss Stilwell.

'What intelligent and resourceful children. They must have a very good teacher,' and Miss Stilwell tries very hard not to smile.

'What. A. Dude,' Benny says, and I am

prouder of Thomas Ernest Blake in that moment than I could possibly say.

16

It is a good thing someone brings the tall ladder
when they do, because Benny's arms are aching
and we are both pretty tired and beginning to
need the loo.

I think the men in the van have gone.

We start climbing down, which is weirdly
a whole lot scarier and harder to do than
climbing up.

Sometimes I dream about trying to get

down from a great height. It is always harder than going up and I usually wake up in a cold sweat. It's always a big relief to remember I'm just at home, in bed, dreaming. This time, it is a big relief to have both feet back on the ground.

Miss Stilwell watches us. Her arms are folded and her mouth is a thin red line. She crouches down so that she is about the same height as we are, maybe smaller.

She says, 'That was foolish and dangerous.' There is a slight tremor in her bottom lip. 'I was very worried for your safety.'

'Sorry,' I say, and Benny looks at the ground.

'You will both be staying in at lunchtime for the rest of the term,' she says. 'We cannot have people just climbing trees in this school.'

'We were trying to save it,' I say.

'Well, you put yourselves at risk.' She shudders. 'I dread to think what might have happened.'

She looks straight at Benny. 'Your mum is not going to be pleased.'

'I know.'

'She's taking you home after lunch. And your mum has been called, Joy. She's on her way to get you.'

I am about to say something about this not being necessary because of Grandad being right here, but he shakes his head at me quickly, in a secret sort of signal, and then pretends to be reading our oak leaf again, so I keep it zipped.

Miss Stilwell says, 'Come inside and get your things. You are both suspended for the rest of the week.'

'It's a thousand years old,' Benny says,

and I feel like hugging him, and Miss Stilwell straightens up and shakes her head and leads the way.

When we get back to 6C, I don't know what to expect, but I brace myself for some new and furious words from Mrs Hunter about what a terrible human being I am. I can tell that everyone in the class has been warned about keeping their mouths shut and their eyes on their work. Nobody moves a muscle.

Mrs Hunter towers over us. She looms like a raincloud. Her shoes look very uncomfortable, like they are strangling her legs.

'I am not impressed,' she says, and we say, 'Sorry.'

'So this is me,' she says, 'telling you off,' and we sort of pause, and say, 'Okay.'

I have no idea where this is going. It is like walking in the dark with no stars and no compass and no map.

'That was very reckless,' she says, and we say, 'Sorry,' again.

'Start a petition,' she tells us. 'Get a tree preservation order,' and we say, '*Sorry?*'

'I didn't tell you that,' she says, and we look at one another and then back at her.

'Get as many names as you can,' she says. 'The nice man from the Historical Society will help you.'

'That's Joy's grandad,' Benny says, and Mrs Hunter's eyes are suddenly as bright and round as marbles, and she tips her head back and lets out a little dog-bark sort of laugh.

17

Our mums are both pretty angry when they come to get us. We have to stand with them and Miss Stilwell at the edge of the playground, just out of reach of the shade of our tree. We have to be very sombre and serious.

'What were you thinking?' Benny's mum says, and mine says, 'Yes, what were you thinking?' like an echo. Then she sees Grandad on the other side of the playground, talking to

Mrs Hunter, and she says, 'What on earth is *he* doing here?'

I say, 'Can we just go?'

Mum's hands are on her hips and she looks really baffled, and Benny's mum is frowning.

'I don't think you get to call the shots right now, Joy Applebloom,' Mum says.

'I really need the loo.'

Benny opens his mouth to say something, and his mum raises a long pointed finger.

'Don't even think about it, Benny Hooper,' she says.

'I'm Rina,' Mum says, and Benny's mum says, 'Angela,' and they shake hands.

Miss Stilwell's brown eyes are like two shiny buttons. She is using words like *irresponsible* and *reckless* and *suspended,* and when she says *consequences,* I know she doesn't mean the fun drawing game.

'Suspended?' Angela says, and she shakes her head at us, and Mum says, 'Really? Oh, for goodness' sake.'

Grandad starts walking over.

Mum starts to introduce him to everybody. 'This is—'

Grandad interrupts. 'Thomas Blake,' he says. 'From the local Historical Society.'

'What?' Mum says, and I tug on her sleeve, and Miss Stilwell frowns and says, 'Yes, we have met.'

After that, Miss Stilwell gets called inside to take a phone call, and the five of us start walking to the gates – Grandad and Mum and Angela and Benny and me. Our signs are leaning up against the tree and the floor is covered in our clever leaves and I swear, for a split second, our mums look at each other, and smile.

'Suspended,' Mum says again. 'How are we supposed to get any work done?'

I look over at Thomas Evergreen Blake, hoping and hoping that Mum will have the same good idea as me.

Grandad must be thinking the same, because straight away he says, 'Can I do anything to help?'

I cross my fingers, really tight. Mum frowns at him. 'What on earth was going on back there?' she said.

Grandad raises his dusty old eyebrows and says something about *merely attending in his official capacity* and Mum rolls her eyes, just like Claude.

'Well, yes, then,' she says. 'You can help. Thanks.'

And to me, she says, 'You can be with your grandad and obey all his rules this week, young lady.'

'Can Benny come?' I say, trying not to sound too enthusiastic.

Mum looks at Angela. 'He's welcome,' she says.

'Are you sure?'

'Of course,' Mum says. 'The more the merrier.' And then behind her hand, she says, 'They'll be glad to get back to school. They won't have that much fun, not with my dad.'

And I don't look at him, because I mustn't. But I know without needing to look that Benny Hooper is doing nothing but smiling, and that between us and the nice man from the Historical Society, we are going to be very, *very* busy.

And then something even better happens. My mum asks Angela if she wants to come back, right now, to 48 Plane Tree Gardens, and have a cup of tea. 'If it's not out of your way,' she says, and she smiles, and Benny's mum smiles back.

They are making friends. I feel it tingling at the ends of my fingers and the edges of my ears.

'Sounds good,' Angela says.

We walk home together, all of us, to 48 Plane Tree Gardens, and my smile is a jaw-breaker.

Benny loves the gate and the storm-cloud grey.

He says, 'You have your own front door. And your own garden. That's amazing.'

He crouches down to tickle Buster behind the ears. He stands up again and shakes hands with my dad. He grins at Claude, who ruffles my hair and offers Benny a biscuit.

It is like a dream come true. Everyday magic, in Grandad's pond-coloured sitting room.

I look at Benny.

'Do you want to go outside and play?' I say.

'Where?'

'In the back garden,' I tell him.

'There's a back garden too?' he says.

'We could look for treasure.'

Benny grins again and finishes his biscuit.

'Definitely. We could.'

And so that is exactly what we do.

Acknowledgements

Thank you, Thank you, THANK YOU to Veronique Baxter (as EVER) and Rachel Denwood, for seeing the silver linings in my work from day one. And Sophie Hartman, for reading early and loving Joy from the very beginning.

All About
JOY

FULL NAME: Joy Applebloom

AGE: 10 years old

PLACE OF BIRTH: Water

HAIR COLOUR: Brick brown

EYE COLOUR: Nut brown

HEIGHT: Short

SIBLINGS: Claude

PETS: Buster, who is Grandad's cat.

BEST FRIEND: Benny Hooper, who is new.

FAVOURITES*

(* I am not sure I have a favourite *anything*
because there are too many possible choices
in the world and I don't think I can pick

only one. So these are firsts, not favourites, because they came out first. They are at the front of the queue in my brain.)

COLOUR: Blue-sky blue

BREAKFAST: Idli (soft steamed rice and lentil cakes from South India) with coconut sambal and fresh tomato chutney. They take eight hours to make and eight seconds to eat.

ANIMAL: Turtle. Maybe.

BIRD: Starling. I have seen thousands and thousands of them flying together, making shapes that look like whales and helter-skelters and giant stingrays in the sky.

PICNIC SANDWICH: Cheese and pickle

TOWN: At the moment I am trying my best to like the one I am in.

TYPE OF TRANSPORT: Tuk-tuks are hilarious. And I really do love being on a boat.

SEASON: Spring. For all the green shoots.

MONTH: I like them all.

NUMBER: 8

TREE: Banyan

SOUND: Rain on a tent. As long as there aren't too many holes.

SMELL: Top-of-a-snowy-mountain air.

If I could be…

ANIMAL: Chameleon. Or an octopus. I am still deciding. One can change colour but the other one has three hearts, nine brains and blue blood. Octopus.

WHAT TREE WOULD YOU BE? A 1,000-year-old oak.

WHAT TIME IN HISTORY WOULD YOU TRAVEL TO? Ancient Egypt? Or maybe the future. Is that allowed?

Look out
for more
JOY

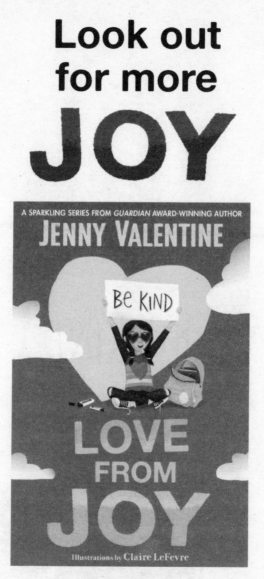

A SPARKLING SERIES FROM *GUARDIAN* AWARD-WINNING AUTHOR

JENNY VALENTINE

BE KIND

LOVE
FROM
JOY

Illustrations by Claire LeFevre

coming soon!

Turn the page for a sneak peek!

Even though I am on the small and cheerful side, I have some big and serious things on my mind. I am juggling them like a clown at the circus and I don't know yet if juggling is one of my special skills.

I have made a list, so I can see how many things I'm supposed to be able keep in the air without dropping.

Number one: Claude has been grounded. This is the end of her actual world.

Two: She is not talking to Mum and Dad. Not one single word. Grandad says this is called sending them to Coventry, and I don't know why it's Coventry's fault, but I do know that I would hate to get the silent treatment from my sister. It would be like getting locked out of a bright room.

Number three: I think Grandad is lonely.

Even his own cat has abandoned him.

Number four: We have mice.

Five: My best friend, Benny, has fallen out with a boy called Chunk.

Six: I am on a mission to get my teacher Mrs Hunter to actually *like* me.

Seven: I am behind on my correspondence. I have a load of letters I need to write and the pile is getting bigger every day.

Big thing number eight is a top-secret plan about a birthday. I can't say one thing about it to a single soul or the secret will spring a leak and I will be a sieve and not a clam. So, for now, I am sending a certain person's birthday surprise to Coventry.

Oh, and number nine: I have started *sleepwalking*.

It is extremely complicated and difficult to

juggle nine things at once, especially when you are also having to be tidy, keep room in your head for school, do your share of the washing-up, not annoy your prickly big sister, make new friends but stay in touch with your old ones, and try your hardest to get your teacher to actually like you. I have watched acrobats in Kazakhstan throw clay pots at each other at the same time as doing one-armed handstands, without one single breakage. I have seen travelling performers in Morocco balance goats on their shoulders and still keep thirteen skittles in the air. So I know that it is possible. I just have to do my best and try.

Claude has been dropping stuff all over the place since she got grounded. Yesterday she broke Grandad's *Home, Sweet Home* cup accidentally-on-purpose, and she is a total butterfingers for bad words. My furious big sister can swear in nine different languages and she is definitely making the most of that talent.

Being grounded means she can't leave the house, apart from for school, and she is not allowed to go on her phone or anything when she gets home again. This is because she has been sneaking around doing a whole lot of fun-sounding stuff she shouldn't, climbing in and out of our bedroom window when she is supposed to be asleep, and telling me that I have to keep my mouth shut so that Mum and Dad and Grandad don't find out.

Except now they have. Because of big thing number nine.

I was dreaming about being in a market. It was covered and hot and cramped and dusty and stacked all the way up to the ceiling with buckets and watermelons and blankets and crates of flowers and huge cuddly toys. It was just like the market we went to in Mumbai, where Claude couldn't stop sneezing because of the spices and her face was all scrunched and quivery like a squirrel's and I laughed till I cried.

In the dream, I wasn't laughing and I wasn't crying either. I was opening and closing hundreds of teeny tiny drawers, searching for who-knows-what, and the drawers were getting teenier and tinier, and harder and harder to open, until my fingers were about as much use as balloons. The next thing I knew, I was waking up in the room I share with Claude in real life. I was out of bed already and standing up in my pyjamas all the way over by the bookcase, and Mum and Dad were there too.

'Wow,' I said. 'Was I *sleepwalking*?'

I started to tell them about the market dream because it was very vivid and still almost real in my head, but they weren't what I would call fascinated.

Dad was leaning halfway out of the window and Mum was saying, 'Where the *hell* has she gone?' meaning my sister, and I had to tell them I didn't know.

They looked scared, and that's not a thing I'm used to seeing, so I said, 'Sorry,' and then they said, 'What? Did you know about this?' and I said, 'Well, yes. Sort of.'

Dad's frown swooped down on me like a vulture and Mum's lips went bone-white. I got back into bed and pulled the sheets up to my neck. There were no nets filled with drying chillies on the ceiling. No umbrellas or jangling cow bells or bicycle wheels. Not like in the market in Mumbai. Not like in my dream.

'And what exactly do you know?' they said, together, at the same time.

'Nothing really,' I said, which was kind of true.

'It's MIDNIGHT,' Dad said, booming like a town clock.

'Has she done this before?' Mum asked, and I said, 'Maybe.'

'Oh, JOY,' Dad boomed again.

'Yes?'

'Why on earth didn't you tell us?'

'Because Claude told me not to.'

Mum shook her head. 'There are some secrets you keep, Joy,' she said, 'and some secrets you don't.'

This was news to me. It actually still is.

'*Really?*' I said. 'How do you tell the

difference? How do you know which is which?'

They didn't answer my question, and Claude didn't answer her phone the fourteen times they rang it either.

'Stay where you are,' they said to me, as if I had done the sleepwalking on purpose, or was thinking about following my sister out of the window. Then they left the room.

I concentrated on the wallpaper. Claude says the design choices at 48 Plane Tree Gardens are enough to keep anyone awake at night. But I have found that if I squint and get up extra close, the flowers that look like cane toads pattern in our bedroom is really quite relaxing. I must have just dropped off when Claude made her big entrance, head first and out of breath in the dark. She landed on the floor with a grunt, the exact moment that Mum and Dad burst in and switched the light on, which was a shock to all of us, and made my eyeballs want to hide in their sockets like crabs in their shells.

'Uh oh,' Claude said, getting up and trying quite hard to look serious. She wobbled a bit, and then she laughed, kind of to herself, like she'd just heard a joke. She smelled of cough sweets and ashtrays and cola, and she blinked and squinted at us in the dazzling light.

Mum took a long deep breath and spoke su-per-slow-ly, counting the spaces between every word. This is a thing that only happens when she is at the very outer limits of the known universe of being cross. It is rare, like a comet or an eclipse, and I think we are witnessing it more than we used to.

'*Where?*' she said, '*Have?*' '*You?*' '*Been?*'

Claude took her trainers off and chucked

them on the floor. 'Out.'

'Out *where*?' Dad said, with his teeth pressed together, hardly opening his mouth, a ventriloquist on stage without a dummy. 'And with whom?'

'*Whom*?' Claude said, and she shrugged her shoulders, and wobbled a bit more. 'Just *out*.'

'Have you been DRINKING?' Mum said, and my sister snort-laughed, and started coughing, and then everyone had another fight. This is something some people in my family have been practising a lot lately, and getting very good at, the same as me and fractions, because practice makes perfect, and I am really already so much better at those.

In between other, louder words, Mum said Claude was abusing her privileges, and Claude said, 'What privileges?'

Dad said Claude had broken their contract and abused their trust and that this was the last, the *very last straw, young lady.*

Claude made a shape like a teapot and said, 'Oh. You think?'

Mum said, 'You are *thirteen,*' and the teapot said, 'So?' It said all it wanted was its *freedom.*

Dad said, 'Freedom is something you *earn.*'

Claude stuck her fingers in her ears and shouted, 'Oh yeah? Really? WHY?' and then Mum threw her hands in the air and stormed out of the room and Dad just stood there like he'd missed the last train and wasn't at all sure what was supposed to happen next.

My sister followed Mum out into the corridor to have the last word. She likes having those. I had my pillow over my ears by then, like a hat, but it was still pretty loud.

She yelled, 'I HATE YOU,' and Mum yelled, 'FINE.'

Then Dad said the thing about Claude being grounded and she squealed like she'd just been stung by a wasp.

I think that's what woke Grandad up.

He came out of his bedroom with his hair fluffed out like a spring cloud and his pyjamas buttoned all the way up to the neck. I could see him through the doorway from where I was sitting in bed. I haven't known Thomas Ernest Blake that long, but sometimes I love him so much my heart feels like popcorn cooking in my chest. I waved at him, the only other not-furious person in the building, but he couldn't see me without his glasses, so he didn't wave back.